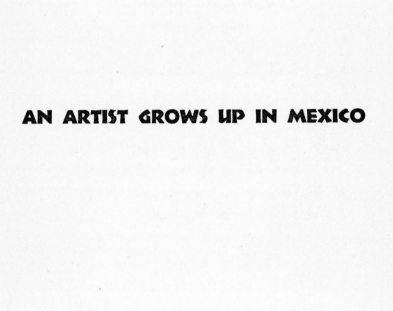

AN ARTIST GROWS UP IN MEXICO

AN ARTIST GROWS UP IN MEXICO

BY
LEAH BRENNER

WITH ILLUSTRATIONS BY DIEGO RIVERA

THE BEECHHURST PRESS

FOREWORD 55227

All of the stories in this book are woven around a boy called Pancho Pacheco who was drawn from the author's imagination. His growth into an artist is purely a product of the imagination and has no relation to the development of any artist living or dead. All of the other characters in the stories are likewise imaginary with the exception of José Guadalupe Posada, one of the greatest Mexican artists. However, the incidents woven around Posada are the product of the author's imagination. Although the stories take place during the dictatorship of Don Porfirio Diaz, it was not intended to give an exact portrayal of that epoch but only a feeling of life in those times. All of the institutions, such as the school of art, are fictitious and suggest no reference to any institutions in Mexico. Lastly, the collaboration between author and artist is entirely artistic and does not represent any shared political belief. The stories were meant to entertain the public in general and are herewith dedicated in loving memory to my father and to Dr. David Glusker of Mexico City.

LEAH BRENNER

ACKNOWLEDGMENTS

My hearty thanks go to:

Miss May Massee, editor of juvenile books, The Viking Press, for permission to publish this book of stories with the accompanying drawings by Diego Rivera.

Miss Charlotte Kohler, editor of *The Virginia Quarterly Review*, who released the copyright for a story and the Rivera drawings that accompanied it, four of which originally appeared in this magazine.

Mr. Richard J. Walsh, president of The John Day Company, who helped me secure permission to publish two rewritten stories, illustrated by Diego Rivera, which appeared in *Asia and the Americas* when Mr. Walsh was editor of this magazine.

Miss Pearl Steinhaus, editor of the *United Nations World*, who gave me a transfer of copyright from the United Nations World, Inc., of the two stories, together with Rivera illustrations, which appeared in *Asia and the Americas*.

Herewith I thank the fine writers Mr. Charles Angoff, Mr. Hiram Hadyn, Mr. James Rorty, and my sister Anita Brenner for encouraging me to bring out my stories.

LEAH BRENNER

New York City
March, 1953

CONTENTS

MOON MAGIC

Moon Magic

MOON MAGIC

Hिगh up in the mountains of Mexico, above the town of Guanajuato, there lived an old Indian witch doctor and her grandchild. The old woman taught her grandchild, whose name was María, how to make simple remedies out of herbs and dead animals. All the Indian peasants, who lived deep in the mountains, went to the witch doctor and her grandchild when they had pains or were cursed by their enemies. María helped the old woman to cure the peasants with natural remedies and to remove their curses with black magic.

When María was fifteen, her grandmother's heart became very weak. Before the old woman passed away, she gave María something that was hundreds of years old which she had buried under the hard dirt floor of their hut. She told María that the thing would talk to her in a man's voice and tell her how to cure sick people. When her grandmother died, María took a long gray flannel skirt, which the old woman had worn, and bundled up the thing in the skirt so that nothing could happen to it.

The next day four Indian peasants carried the rude box, which held the old woman's body, to a hill far away from the hut. Behind the peasants walked a fat priest in a black robe that flapped at his heels. María and the peasants' wives walked behind the priest with black shawls wrapped around

13

their heads and their long colored skirts blowing in the wind. When the wives told María that her grandmother's death made them sad, she only said, "The death of my grandmother had to come. Each one of us must die."

María did not let her words show any sorrow over her grandmother's death because the old woman had taught her to hide her feelings of grief and fear. None of the peasants' wives could tell by looking at María's brown face how she felt about the death. María had no tears in her black eyes while she walked to her grandmother's funeral and her pink mouth was set firmly under her long nose. Yet she felt the loss of her grandmother so deeply that her body ached from the anguish in her bosom.

The sun shone on her two black braids, which hung below her shawl, while she watched the peasants dig a hole for her grandmother's body. When the priest began to pray, "May the soul of this woman rest in heaven . . . " María shut her eyes because she believed that her grandmother's soul would go to the paradise of Lord Tlaloc, the god of rain whom her ancestors had worshiped. At the end of the prayers, María gave the priest a few silver pesos since it was the custom for him to bury the dead and be paid.

After the old woman was buried, Indian men and women, with brown babies strapped to their backs, came to María when they were ill. She listened to the peasants' stories about their ailments and then asked the thing, bundled up in the gray flannel skirt, how to cure them. All the peasants stared curiously at the gray bundle and waited for it to tell María how to cure them. When they did not hear any voice come from the bundle, they began to imagine that it held something which only spoke to María's mind.

The peasants gave María a little money or a chicken after

she cured them with the help of the bundle. None of them mentioned the bundle to her, but they walked away from her hut talking about it. They used to say, "The bundle is round and must hold a round thing . . . but it could not be a squash because a squash can not talk . . . who knows what is in the bundle. . . ."

As time went on, the feeling grew within María that it was her life to cure the peasants. She loved to feed tiny babies a few spoonfuls of herb tea for their colic. Every time she cured a man, woman, or child, she felt that she could not have done it unless the thing in the gray bundle had told her what to do. The thing became more and more valuable to her. Whenever she left her hut alone, she hid the bundle for fear that some bad peasant might steal the sacred thing which her grandmother had inherited.

The old woman had been dead five years when María heard loud knocks on her door one winter night. She opened the door and saw two peasants who were strangers to her. One of them had a brown *sarape*, which smelled of pigs, wrapped around his head and body. The other peasant wore a sombrero pushed down on his head and had an old white cloth rolled over his ears.

"*Mujer*," the peasant who stank of pigs said to María in a rough voice, "woman, my friend has pains in his ears and needs a cure."

María nodded and told the men to come into her hut. It had one small room that was bare of furniture. A straw mat lay on its dirt floor. Dead snakes, bunches of herbs, and rabbit skins were dangling from the roof. A clay pot of herb tea was brewing on a charcoal brazier in a corner. The gray bundle and some clay jars were lying near the fire.

A coyote howled in the night when María crouched down

on the ground beside the bundle. She placed the palms of her hands on it and prayed fervently in Spanish, *"Espíritu sagrado . . .* holy spirit of the god of my ancestors . . . Lord Tlaloc . . . please tell me what kind of remedy I should use to cure this man."

She cocked her head over the bundle and listened to it for a few minutes. Then she whirled around and told the peasant, whose ears ached, to lie down on the straw mat. She picked up a clay jar of snake fat, knelt beside him and gently rubbed a little fat in his ears with her fingers.

The pigman watched and thought: The bundle contained something, which belonged to Lord Tlaloc, that had told the woman how to cure his friend. . . .

María heated two flat stones on the fire and slipped out a small knife from the waist of her skirt. She cut a rabbit skin in half, wrapped the hot stones in the skins, and laid them against the peasant's ears.

The peasant fell asleep and began to snore. When he work up and felt no more pain, he mumbled, *"Gracias, Doña María."* He rose clumsily to his feet, pulled some copper coins out of a knotted rag, and gave them to her.

The pigman stared greedily at the bundle and thought: If he owned what is in the bundle, it would tell him how to cure sick men and women . . . he could make people give him money for curing them . . . he would take the bundle home and use it like the woman. . . . He looked at María, while she was tucking the copper coins in her bosom, and said to himself: She would not see me if I put the bundle under my *sarape* and sneaked out of the hut. . . .

When the pigman laid his hands on the bundle, María raised her eyes. She slipped out her knife, ran toward him, and stabbed his right arm. He drew out of his sash a small

16

machete, which he used to cut up corn to feed his pigs, and slashed her chin. The other peasant yelled, *"Mal hombre!"* as he grabbed the machete away from the pigman. He ran out of the hut, and the peasant chased him down the mountain path with the machete in his hand.

María washed off the wound on her chin with the herb tea that was brewing on the fire. Then she lay down on the straw mat with the bundle beside her. She tossed on the straw mat all night long and thought: The pigman might come back and try to steal her bundle again . . . if he took the thing, she could not cure any more peasants . . . but she would run away before he came back and attacked her for the bundle . . . she would go down to the town of Guanajuato and work in some house where she could hide her bundle.

At the break of day María threw her clothes into a corn sack and put a little food in a rag. She picked up the bundle, piled some thorny branches against the door of the hut, and untied her old burro. She roped the sack on its rump and was about to rope the bundle on the sack when she thought: If she tied the bundle on the burro, the thing might fall off the beast and break . . . the pieces could not tell her how to cure the peasants.

She climbed on the burro with the bundle in her left arm and sat down sideways. Her long faded pink skirt billowed around her legs, but her feet were bare and brown as earth. As she kicked the burro with her heels to make it start, she wished that she could kick and beat the pigman. She muttered, "It is all on account of him that I must leave my hut. . . ." Tears came to her eyes when she glanced up from the burro and looked at the hut.

It was a primitive hut built from rocks laid together with mud to keep out the rain and cold. Mountain grass was piled on top of the roof which had been made from bamboo and light tree trunks. Behind the hut stood a little room which María used for a kitchen. The hut was encircled by a rock wall, covered with thorny branches, to protect it from wild animals.

María cried out excitedly, *"Arre, burro!* Get along, donkey!"

She held the bundle in her lap while the burro plodded down a path that was surrounded by trees and magueyes. It was the only path which led through the mountains to Guanajuato, but the burro knew the path because María rode down to the town to buy things in the market. She grumbled, "I have lived up here in the mountains all my life . . . if it were not for the pigman, I would not have to go live in Guanajuato now and hide my bundle. . . ."

Toward noon she untied the rag in which she had put a little beans and rice and ate them slowly. After awhile she leaned over the burro to see whether she could get a glimpse of Guanajuato. It lay in a valley, hundreds of feet beneath her, and she could not even see the church spires in the town. For the rest of the day she sat quietly on the burro and meditated while it trudged down the narrow path that wound through the mountains.

It was dusk when María passed the silver mines on the outskirts of Guanajuato. She rode up and down the hilly roads in the town until she came to an inn for peasants where she left her burro. She slung the corn sack over her shoulder and carried the gray bundle in her arm as she set off to look for work. When she reached a narrow road called the Alley of Dead Dogs, she knocked on the door of an adobe house that was painted soft pink.

A tall dark man came to the door and asked, "What do you wish?"

"I," said María, "come in search of work."

He thought a minute and said, "My wife is delicate and we need someone to help her take care of our little boy."

María was curious and she asked, "What is the name of the boy?"

He stroked his black beard and smiled. "We named him Francisco Pacheco, after me, but we call him Pancho."

"It would give me pleasure," she said, "to take care of little Pancho."

"Where," Señor Pacheco asked, "do you come from?"

María pointed to the mountains and replied "From my hut. . . ." She closed her lips tight and would not tell him that she was a witch doctor.

"Well," he said slowly, "I think that you can take care of Pancho."

He led María into a patio that had an old well in it. Across from the patio stood a small dark room furnished with a chest of drawers, a rocking chair, and a bamboo cradle. María leaned over the cradle and peered at Pancho while he slept. He had black eyes, a tiny pug nose, and full red cheeks. She loved his face at sight, and she exclaimed under her breath, "How pretty he is!"

"Now," Señor Pacheco said, "I will leave you alone with my son."

María sat down on her knees beside the cradle and watched Pancho. When he turned his head and woke up screaming, she picked him up. Holding him against her breasts, she kissed and hugged him until he became quiet.

That night María lay down on the floor at the foot of Pancho's cradle. When she could not hear any noise in the

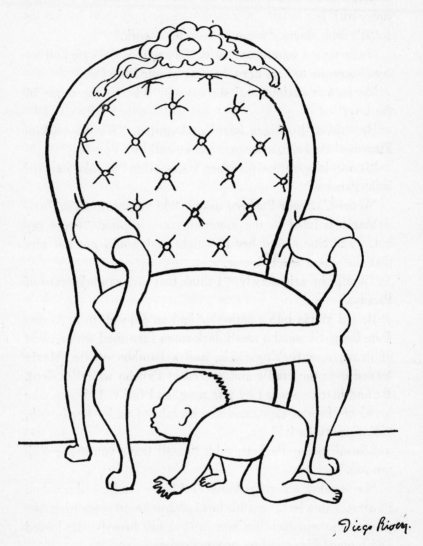

Pancho crawled under the big chair in the parlor

house, she went into the patio with her bundle. She dug a hole, with her hands, in a corner of the patio and buried the bundle in it. Then she ran back to Pancho's room.

Days rolled by slowly while María took care of Pancho. She began to feel as if he were her own son because she was alone with him most of the time. She fed the child, bathed him, and sat beside his cradle while his mother rested because of her delicate health. María was so busy taking care of Pancho that the pigman faded out of her mind. She loved the boy more and more as the days grew into weeks, months, and finally one year.

When Pancho started to talk, he held out his arms to María and called, "Marí-aa . . . Marí-aa. . . ." He loved María and cried when his mother took him away from her.

Pancho was two years old when his mother became very ill and the family doctor came to see her. The doctor prescribed some medicines for her and went into the parlor to talk to Pancho's father. There was a big chair in the parlor, and Pancho was crawling under it when the doctor saw him. The little boy looked so pale and flabby to the doctor that he said to his father, "I believe Pancho needs a change of climate. I think that he should be taken up in the mountains."

When the doctor rode away on his horse, Señor Pacheco called María before him and said, "You told me, on the day you came here, that you had a hut in the mountains. Would you take my boy away to it for a few weeks or so?"

She nodded and cried, *"Sí, señor!"*

María and Pancho rode out of Guanajuato on a day in August in the year 1888 on a mule. She sat sideways on the beast, and Pancho was strapped to her back in her black shawl. Both of them wore sombreros to shade their eyes from the sun. María's old burro plodded along behind them. Its

21

María took Pancho away to her hut in the mountains

sides were loaded with two wooden crates full of corn, beans, rice, dried meat, candles, blankets, Pancho's clothes, and some clay pots.

María had dug up the bundle at midnight and had packed it in a bed of straw at the top of one of the crates. She was full of joy because she was going back to her hut, and she sang out at the mule, *"Andale, mula!* Hurry up, mule!" The mule swished its tail while it walked down the long road that led to the mountain pass. Pancho stared at a few Indian peasants who came down the road with a load of corn or wheat on their backs.

An old peasant jogged down the road on a burro. He kicked the beast in its belly, rode up to María, and took off his sombrero.

"Muy buenos días, Doña María," he said.

She bowed to him from the mule.

The old man twisted his sombrero in his hands and said, "Someone has put a curse on my grandchild. I will bring her to you soon for a cure."

María said, "May all go well with you until then."

"Many thanks!" the old man cried. He kicked the burro, put on his sombrero, and jogged down the road toward Guanajuato.

María turned into the narrow path that wound through the mountains. It had rained the night before and the path was covered with soft mud. The mule and burro were plowing their way through the mud when a herd of pigs came down the path. They began to wallow in the mud, and the mule and burro could not get past them. María sat and waited patiently for the Indian who was driving the herd to make the pigs move out of the way.

The Indian pushed his sombrero to the back of his head as

he walked slowly down the path. He broke into a run when Pancho held his nose and screamed, "The pigs stink! Get them out of the way!" The Indian shouted, *"Ahorita!* Right now!" and looked up at Pancho. María turned her face away when she saw that it was the man who had tried to steal her bundle.

He beat the pigs with a stick and yelled, *"Huche, cochinos!* Hurry up, pigs!" They shook the mud off their backs and ran past the mule and burro. María glanced over her shoulder at the pigman as she rode up the path. He was swinging his stick in the air and trotting along behind the pigs.

She fingered the scar on her chin from the machete wound and thought suspiciously: The pigman did not seem to recognize her . . . but who knows . . . he might have remembered her . . . maybe he pretended that he had forgotten her . . . and did not attack her because he did not think she had the bundle with her.

The pigman took all the joy out of her going home, and she became gloomier and gloomier as the day passed. When she looked at the dark gray clouds in the sky, she was full of forebodings about returning to the hut with her bundle. Rain began to fall when she rode up to the hut late in the afternoon. She slid off the mule, took the bundle out of the crate, and hurried into the hut with Pancho so that he would not get wet.

As she unstrapped him from her back, she stared at the old straw mat on the floor and thought: She would roll up her bundle in the straw mat to hide it from the pigman in case he came to the hut and tried to steal it. . . .

Pancho pointed to the bundle and asked, "What is in that?"

"It is a secret," she said and rolled up her bundle in the straw mat.

He pouted and cried out, "But I want to see what is in it!"
She shook her head at him.

"Tell me the secret," he begged, "tell me, María. . . ."

María kissed the child and put him to sleep in a large
basket. She lay down on the floor but could not sleep. Toward
dawn she heard loud raps on her door. Pancho woke up when
she screamed, "Who is outside?"

A man shouted in a gruff old voice, "A friend!"

María opened the door and saw a crowd of peasants. One
of them was the old man whom she had met on the road. He
said, "I hope that you will pardon me, Doña María, for com-
ing so early with my family. But my grandchild," he nodded
at a young girl wrapped in a blue shawl, "needs a cure."

"Please come in," María said, "my home is yours."

All the peasants crowded around María to shake her hand.
She smiled as she gave her hand to the wife of the old man,
the mother of the girl, and her future husband. The women
took off their shawls and the future husband fingered his
sombrero while the old man handed María a chicken, two
fish, and a basket of eggs covered with a napkin. He said, "I
brought you a few things, Doña María, to pay you for remov-
ing a curse from my grandchild."

She thanked him and asked, "Who cursed her?"

"A woman!" the old man growled." She is jealous of my
grandchild's future husband. The woman screamed at my
grandchild, 'May your eyes fall out before you get married
to the man I love!' My grandchild's right eyelid has been
jerking ever since the woman cursed her."

María said, "I can rid your grandchild of the curse, but
we must wait until tonight because the moon will help me to
cure her with magic."

The old man scratched his head and said, *"Pos . . . well. . . ."*

And the day went by in conversation. Pancho played with the young girl while the peasants talked to María about the rain and their crops of corn and beans. When the sun went down, she built a fire and put a clay pot of herb tea on to brew. Then she poured some water into a squash gourd and set it beside the straw mat in which she had rolled up the bundle.

The peasants became fearful when María was about to begin the cure. They believed that evil spirits would come into the hut and harm them while she removed the curse. The old man put on his big sombrero to keep evil spirits away from him, and the future husband imitated him. All the women wrapped their shawls around their heads and squatted on the dirt floor.

When the moon rose above the mountains, María placed the palms of her hands on the straw mat and prayed: "Holy spirit of the god of my ancestors . . . Lord Tlaloc . . . please tell me how to cure this girl with magic. . . ." She cocked her head over the straw mat and listened to the bundle. All of a sudden she pulled a dead snake down from the roof and grabbed two eggs.

Holding the eggs in her hands, she knelt down and made the girl kneel before her. She whispered, "An evil spirit is making the eyelid jerk . . . the evil spirit came with the curse of the woman. . . ." As she stroked the eyelid with each egg, she mumbled over and over, "May the eggs suck up the evil spirit. . . ." Cracking the eggs in the squash gourd, she chanted, "The eggs sucked up the evil spirit . . . may it sink into the water with the eggs. . . ."

She wrapped the dead snake around her hand and rubbed

Pancho watched María cure the young girl

the eyelid with its head. Then she dipped a rag in the herb tea, washed off the eye, and said gently, "My child, your eyelid will jerk no more."

María's voice soothed the girl and made all the fear, which had upset her when she was cursed by the woman, leave her.

The old man looked at his grandchild and shouted, "Her eyelid is not jerking now! Doña María rid her of the curse!"

The peasants crowded around María to congratulate her. She was so happy that she cried out, "Please sit on my mat instead of the dirt!" She unrolled the straw mat, kissed Pancho, and let him sit near the bundle.

When the peasants sat down on the straw mat, María said, "The hour has come for us to celebrate!" She went out to the little room behind the hut and looked for her jug of *mezcal*. Within a few minutes she came back into the hut with her arm wrapped around the jug. When she glanced at Pancho, she squeezed the jug to her breasts until the muscles in her arm showed.

Pancho had undone the bundle, and he was playing with the sacred thing which her ancestors had made hundreds of years ago. He burst out laughing as he hurled the thing on the ground to see if it would break.

María's heart pounded as she fell on her knees beside the pieces. Her mind was full of anguish and pain spread through her body while she cried to herself: "I can not cure any more sick people . . . because the spirit of Lord Tlaloc will never talk to me again . . . and tell me how to cure them . . . his spirit was in his head . . . and the child has broken his head. . . ."

Pancho pointed at the pieces of a long nose and two heads of snakes that were carved around the mouth of Lord Tlaloc and said, *"La cabeza era de barro . . . nada más . . .* the head was only clay. . . ."

María's head whirled as she rose up on her knees and raised her hands to strike the child who had destroyed her life. Her eyes fell on his face which she loved. She sank back on her knees and her hands slipped to her sides. Her face was so impassive that the peasants could not tell any tragedy had befallen her when she said to Pancho, "Yes, it was only clay."

THE GHOST'S SHOES

THE GHOST'S SHOES

ONCE UPON A TIME there lived an Indian girl whose name was Paz. Her feet were brown and hard because she always went barefoot and had never owned a pair of shoes in her life. She usually wore a yellow cotton blouse and an old rose-colored skirt that reached to her ankles. When it was cool, she wrapped a deep blue shawl around her head and shoulders. Her long black hair fell in two braids down her back.

Her face was neither brown nor white but the color of dark copper. When she became frightened, her high cheekbones turned pale. The expression on her face, most of the time, was so calm that her eyes, nose, and mouth looked as if they were carved. She had black eyes shaped like almonds, a long nose that was broad around the nostrils, and full lips.

Paz lived with her father in an adobe hut on a hill above the town of Guanajuato. Her father was a poor old man called José. He had some white hair on his chin, and his back was bent from carrying a heavy basket. The old man was a peon in a silver mine. He lugged the ore, which other men dug up, out of the mine in a big basket on his back.

When the sun fell, José was tired. He walked homewards with some men who labored in silver mines around the town. When he arrived at the adobe hut, he found Paz in the shed

33

behind it. She was sitting on her knees, stirring a pot of beans on a charcoal brazier. A jug of water, some clay dishes, and a pile of tortillas wrapped in a faded purple rag were on the ground.

Paz turned her head. "Good evening, papa."

He mumbled, "Good evening, daughter."

The old man sat down on the hard earth and took off his sombrero. He felt cool and kept on the brown blanket that slipped over his head and fell below the knees of his cotton pants. As he waited for Paz to give him food, he scratched his head as though something were on his mind.

"Your supper, papa." She gave him a bowl of beans and the tortillas in the faded purple rag.

Old José grunted his thanks. He ripped a tortilla in half, dipped it in his beans, and ate.

Paz did not eat until she gave him a mug of coffee. She waited on her father the way her mother had waited on him when she was alive.

Old José rarely said more than a few words while he ate, but this evening he was particularly quiet. Some of his friends who worked with him in the mine had told him that a lot of treasure was buried in the town. When he finished the coffee, he wiped his mouth on the sleeve of his soiled white blouse and sat thinking about the buried treasures.

As it was growing dark, Paz lit a candle stuck in a bottle. She threw the deep blue shawl over her shoulders and waited for her father to talk a little while before he lay down to sleep.

The old man picked his teeth with a match-stick and began to think out loud by telling Paz what his friends had told him.

"A long time ago," he said very slowly, "many people became rich from the silver in the mines around our town. When there was a war or a revolution, these rich people were afraid of being robbed of their money and jewelry, so they hid them in the houses where they lived. Many put their gold and precious jewels in chests or clay jars and buried them under the floors, behind the walls, or in secret places in their houses."

The old man gazed vacantly at a fly buzzing around the pot of beans and said, "A number of people died suddenly or were killed before they could remove their wealth. For this reason, a lot of money and jewelry has been found in old houses where the rich people lived."

Paz looked down at her bare feet and wished that she could find a buried treasure and buy herself a pair of shoes.

"There are nights when," her father lowered his voice, "ghosts of the rich people appear before a person who is living in their houses. The ghosts want to show this person where their treasures are hidden and they knock like this," he rapped his hand, "on the hiding-places."

Paz had been afraid of ghosts all her life. She glanced fearfully at her father out of the corners of her almond eyes and asked, "Why do the ghosts want somebody to know where they buried their wealth?"

Old José whispered, "Evil spirits will not let the rich people rest in their graves because they hid their treasures. When ghosts of the rich people knock on the hiding-places, they give away their wealth and return to their graves forever because evil spirits let them rest in peace."

Paz stared at her father and said nothing. She was so frightened of the ghosts that her mind darkened. Her face did not reveal any fear because she rarely showed her feelings. Only her copper cheekbones flushed a little when she became excited and thought: If a ghost ever came to tell her where his treasure was buried, she would run away.

A gentle wind blew through the door of the shed and made the candle flicker. The old man picked up his sombrero and pushed it down on his head because he believed that night air was bad for his ears. He said, "I would not have to work in the mine if I found some money."

"Wouldn't you be afraid of the ghost who let you see where it was hidden?"

"A bit." He pulled the white hair on his chin and reflected. "But these ghosts do not resemble ordinary ghosts."

"No, papa?"

He shook his head. "These ghosts are dressed up in the clothes they wore many years ago when they were rich people."

Her black eyes opened wide as she watched him describe the ghosts.

Putting a hand on his brim, he said, "The ghosts do not carry straw sombreros like mine but costly felt hats made in Europe. Instead of wearing a brown blanket like me, they have on expensive black coats or capes. The clothes of the lady ghosts are even more luxurious. They wear silk dresses with ribbons and lace and rare flowers in their hair."

Old José meditated. "I heard," he said in a faraway voice, "that all the ghosts look very strange because they have no faces. Their hats seem to rest in the air. I believe the ghosts are ashamed to show their faces because they hid their money when they were rich people."

The old man talked until the candle burned low in the bottle. He stood up and went out to a field behind the shed. When he returned, he lay down on his straw mat and fell asleep.

As Paz lay down to sleep, pictures of ghosts floated through her mind. She heard a dog howl in the night and imagined

the animal was howling because it had seen a ghost without
a face. In her terror her body stiffened and felt numb. Sleep
only came when she listened to the breathing of her father
nearby.

The old man became so tired of working in the mine that
all he desired was to find some buried money. He knew that
other persons in the town had found bags and chests of
money, and he talked about them to Paz for many evenings.
Once he told her that a shoemaker was hammering on a sole
when a ghost appeared and rapped on part of the floor. The
shoemaker dug under the floor and found an ox-skin full of
gold coins.

There came an evening when José did not return to the hut
and talk with Paz. For that afternoon a huge rock fell on him
and crushed his body while he was carrying silver out of the
mine in the basket upon his back. Paz cried and cried until
the lids of her almond eyes were swollen.

Someone told the godmother of Paz about the sad fate of
her father. The godmother visited Paz, and they talked for
many hours. Finally they decided that Paz should go to the
town and search for work. And the godmother said that she
would stay in the hut while Paz was gone.

That night Paz tossed from side to side on her straw mat as
though something were troubling her mind. Once she woke
up and saw only darkness around her. She felt alone when
she thought: Her father was dead. She dropped off to sleep
thinking: What would become of her?

At dawn she awoke and slipped off the straw mat to pre-
pare for her journey. She had saved a few copper coins in a
clay mug, and she put them in her bosom. Two hard tortillas
and a piece of goat cheese were left from yesterday, and she
tied them in the faded purple rag.

As she wrapped her blue shawl around her head, she remembered her father had said, "We are poor and humble, but we have a little home." She twisted her hands anxiously and wondered how she would be able to live without her father. Tears came to her eyes because she was leaving the only home she had ever known. She dropped her eyes to hide the tears and walked slowly out of the hut with her chin drooping sadly.

When she climbed down the hill which led to the town, she raised her head. Her face looked so devoid of feeling that it appeared to be wooden because she would not let herself show any sorrow. Had someone passed her on the road, he would never have guessed that she was suffering.

Upon her arrival at the bottom of the hill, she went down a road that led to the market. Many women with black shawls around their heads were crowded in a butcher shop. Paz saw a skinny yellow dog run into the shop and do something which made all the women exclaim and hold their noses.

She walked to a long cobblestone road that was on a hill. Tall narrow houses painted light rose, green, blue, yellow, or cream lined both sides of the road. When Paz gazed upwards, it seemed that each house stood higher upon the hill and was on top of the house below.

Paz climbed up and up the hill and knocked on the doors of houses. A lady or a child or a servant answered and said they had no work for her. She reached the top of the hill and followed a winding road. It was early in the afternoon and she felt unhappy because she could not find any work. Her body seemed heavier with each step.

She saw a fountain and sat down on the edge. As she wiped the sweat off her copper face with her shawl, she sighed, *"Ay, dios"* and pulled the faded purple rag out of her skirt. She had no thoughts while she munched a stale tortilla and goat cheese. The sudden death of her father and the necessity to look for work had been too much. She sat, long after she finished her food, staring vacantly into space.

When the sun went down, she rose to her feet and walked to a narrow road which bore the sign "Alley of Dead Dogs." There was a pink house at the corner, and she knocked on the door.

A lady with dark hair braided around her head asked, "What do you want, girl?"

"Pardon me," said Paz humbly, "but I am searching for work."

The lady hesitated. "I have a servant, but she is very ill." She held the door open. "You may come in."

Paz stepped into a patio that seemed gloomy after having been in the sun all day. When she raised her eyes, she saw an old rock well in the center of the patio. A water jar lay on the ground with a long rope that was tied to an iron ring at the edge of the well. Lilies and roses were growing around a gnarled old tree whose branches shaded the patio.

The lady went into a hall that separated the patio from the rest of the house. "My name is," she paused, "Señora Pacheco."

Paz nodded her chin and followed the señora through the hall which led to an old-fashioned kitchen. There was a large charcoal brazier made of rose stone and fancy tiles beside the wall. Big and small clay pots were hanging above the brazier. A barrel of water stood nearby.

Paz saw a boy sitting at a table and eating a bowl of rice. His black hair fell in a bang over his forehead, and his face was the color of a pecan. His white teeth showed as he looked up curiously at Paz.

"This child," said the señora, "is my son."

He cried out to Paz, "Good afternoon!"

His greeting made her feel welcome. She replied, "Good afternoon."

Señora Pacheco said, "Do me the favor of washing those dishes." She pointed to some dirty clay pots and the barrel of water.

Paz said meekly, "I will do as you bid." She bundled up her shawl and put it on the brazier as the señora left the room.

The boy held his spoon in the air and asked, "What is your name?"

"Paz," she said simply.

He asked in a high voice, "Don't you wish to know my name?"

"Surely."

"My name is Francisco, but the whole world calls me Pancho. Very soon I will be six years old. How old are you?"

"I am twelve years old, said my papa."

"Where is your papa?"

"He died."

"What a pity!"

Paz began to love Pancho because he was sympathetic.

He said, "My papa teaches school and all the boys like him very much."

That night a profound sorrow filled Paz when she picked up a candle and some blankets, which the señora gave her, and went to a small room in back of the house where she was to sleep. The room had a straw mat on the floor and a picture of the Virgin of Guanajuato on the wall. The ceiling was streaked from rain that had leaked through the roof.

As Paz lay down to sleep, she wished that she were lying on the floor of her adobe hut. For awhile she felt afraid be-

cause she would sleep in a strange room. She began to feel
more secure when she remembered how nice Pancho had been.
At last she fell asleep and dreamed that she was in the hut
with her beloved father.

When she woke up and saw the room around her, she
mourned again. In the clear light of day she realized that her
father was dead and she would have to work in this house.
She wished that she were back in the dream with him on her
way to the kitchen.

Pancho was playing with some dishes on the table and he
cried, "Paz, I am glad that you are here!" He squeezed her
hand.

Since the day of her father's death, Paz had been a lost
soul. She was glad that Pancho wanted her in his house, and
she murmured affectionately, "Panchito, Panchito!"

All morning long Pancho followed her around the house
while she worked. She had no time to think of her father because of Pancho. He made her laugh and talk with him and
forget her grief. In that morning she gave Pancho the love
which she had given to her father.

Late in the afternoon the señora told Paz to sit in the patio
with Pancho while she went to visit some friends. Pancho ran
into his room for a tablet and said, "I am going to draw."

Paz sat down on the ground near the old rock well.

Pancho turned the pages of his tablet. "Don't you want to
see the pictures I have drawn?"

"With pleasure!"

He explained, "They are mountains. I like to draw the
mountains around our town so much."

Paz stared curiously at the mountains.

"And this is how I drew the well."

Paz glanced at his picture of the well in the patio.

He looked her in the face and talked. "One time I heard my mama tell my aunt that a Spaniard built this house with the well. The Spaniard was old and rich because he owned a silver mine. It happened that he became ill and lay in his bed for days without saying a word. One night a rattle came from his throat and he said to his wife, 'Money hidden in the house.' She asked 'Where?' The rattling noise grew louder and he died."

Paz nodded understandingly. She knew from her father that some rich people died suddenly and left money hidden in their houses.

"My mama said the Spaniard was a miser who hoarded all his money because he did not trust any bank. After the funeral, his wife searched the house for money. She looked between their mattress and under the floors and behind the walls and even in this patio. But the old woman could not find a centavo, and one day she passed away in her sleep."

Pancho chewed his pencil reflectively. "Even the servant who used to work for us said that money is hidden in this house! She told me that the Spaniard has a ghost who comes in the night and wants to show one of us where he buried his money."

Paz cried, "Ay!" Her almond eyes darted to the door and she wanted to run away before the ghost came to see her some night.

Pancho felt that something was amiss and he asked, "What is wrong?"

"Nothing." She pressed her lips together and would not tell him that she was afraid of the ghost.

"Really?"

As she looked at his face to give him assurance, her fear

of the ghost subsided. Her love for Pancho was so strong that it overcame the fear and made her stay with him.

"I wish," he said, "I could find the money that is buried in this house. Then I could buy a paint-box to color my mountains. My papa can't buy me one now because the kind I want comes from Europe and costs too much. If I had the paint-box, I would paint my mountains in lovely colors and make them beautiful for you."

She put her arms around him and murmured, "You are very good."

"Now I am going to draw!" He lay down on his belly and drew mountains with softly rounded tops like the mountains around the town.

Every afternoon the señora left Pancho at home with Paz and went to visit her friends. As Paz and Pancho were alone for many days, they became fonder of each other and more dependent upon the other for love.

Spring passed and brought the wet season with rains that were heavier than in other years. One night there was a storm and water dripped through the roof of the small room where Paz slept. She had a sore throat and sneezed in the morning when she went to the kitchen.

The señora heard Paz snuffling and said, "I think the mason is to blame for your cold because he did not fix the holes in the roof. My husband will return late tonight from a dinner at his school, but he should call the mason tomorrow. You must sleep tonight in the hall."

After supper Paz rolled her blankets in her straw mat and carried it to the hall that separated the house from the patio. She was ill from her cold and fell asleep at once. In the wee hours of the morning, she was awakened by some knocks on the main door. She thought it must be the señor returning from the dinner. Half asleep, she opened the door.

A man wearing a wide-brimmed black hat stepped into the patio. His hat was resting in the space above his long black cape. When Paz saw that he had no face, her heart beat faster. Her high cheekbones turned white as she realized: He is a ghost.

He wore black shoes that made no sound while he walked to the old rock well. His full cape spread out like a buzzard's wings as he stooped over the iron ring to which the rope of the water jar was tied. The mind of Paz slipped down into dark unconscious fear when she watched the ghost rap on the iron ring. With his long bony fingers, he pointed to the ground below the edge of the well and beckoned at Paz to come here. Terrified, she ran out of the house and into the night.

As she fled she thought: He was the ghost of the rich Spaniard. The face of Pancho flashed before her eyes. She wanted to run back to him but was horrified of meeting the ghost. A loose cobblestone in the road tripped her foot and made her fall down. She looked up to see a night watchman with a lantern chasing her. In a panic that he might take her to jail, she raced toward a road which led into the mountains.

That morning Pancho and his mother waited in the kitchen for Paz. She did not come for breakfast, and they went to see if she were sick on her straw mat. Since there was no sign of Paz in the hall, the señora imagined that she had run away with a man during the night. The señora asked Pancho if he ever saw Paz with a sweetheart. Pancho shook his head and felt that Paz had deceived him by keeping her man a secret.

With the passing of the days, Pancho missed Paz more because she gave him love. He thought she had abandoned him for her sweetheart, and he was miserable and lonesome.

When he drew pictures of mountains, they seemed no good. He raged at his drawings, tore them up, and ran from the house. As he climbed a hill and gazed at the mountains around the town, they looked beautiful and made him feel that his mountains were ugly.

It rained until autumn brought dry and sunny days. When Pancho asked his mother if she had any news of Paz, the señora clicked her tongue and exclaimed, "Who knows where she went!"

Paz was hiding at a small farm in the mountains where she earned her beans by working on the land. She loved Pancho and wanted to be with him but was afraid the ghost would come back to see her if she returned. She knew that the ghost had rapped on the iron ring and pointed to the ground because his fortune was buried there. Being loyal by nature, she felt that the riches belonged to Pancho since he was the son of the house.

As time went by and he was not in her life anymore, she began to think of her father again. She recalled many things the old man had told her about ghosts when she was by herself at night in a shack on the farm. One winter night as she was sitting in the shack, feeling alone in the world, she could hear her father saying in her mind, "When ghosts of the rich people knock on the hiding-places, they give away their wealth and return to their graves forever."

Paz sat and thought about these words hour after hour. She believed in her father as much in death as in life, and she knew from him that the ghost would now rest in his grave because he had rapped on the iron ring. When her fear of meeting the ghost was gone, she felt a powerful love for the boy whom she left behind. She was lonely on the farm, and it seemed that she heard her father say, "Go back to him."

At the break of day Paz thought: It is my duty to tell Pancho. She put on her shawl, walked out of the shack, and left the farm as quietly as she had come in this night. She saw the owner of the farm on a field but, without saying a word to him, started down the long road that led to the town. Her mind was on the treasure in the well, which should belong to Pancho, and she had no thoughts for anyone else.

A burro loaded with wood ran down the road with its hoofs kicking up dust. A barefoot boy in gray rags trotted behind it waving a stick. Paz slipped her hand in her skirt and pulled out the faded purple rag which she had saved carefully. She held the rag over her mouth and nose to keep the dust from blowing into her face as she went along the road.

Paz was hungry when she arrived in the town at noon. She walked to the cobblestone road on a hill and climbed to the top. Following the winding road, she passed the fountain and reached the narrow road called Alley of Dead Dogs where she knocked on the door of the old pink house.

Pancho answered the door. When he saw Paz, he laughed and threw his arms around her. "I am so happy to see you! Where have you been?"

Paz dropped her eyes from shame because she had run away.

"I am eating," he said. "Let us go to the kitchen."

She accompanied him.

"Have you eaten?"

"No, señor!"

He filled a bowl with soup and gave it to her.

Hungry as she was, Paz could not eat until she told him about the ghost's visit. Her almond eyes became solemn when she explained how the ghost had rapped on the iron ring at the edge of the well and pointed to the ground where his treasure was buried. She ended humbly, "As you are the son of the house, you have the right to the riches in the well."

"What a miracle!" he cried as the door opened and his parents came in the kitchen. "There is a lot of wealth buried in this house!"

Señor and Señora Pacheco stared at their son while he repeated what Paz had told him word for word.

"Who knows if it is the truth?" the señor asked, uncertainly.

The señora argued, "I know and the aunt of Pancho knows that many people have found treasures buried in old houses. We always suspected that the miserly Spaniard hoarded his fortune here."

"You sound like the boys at my school," Señor Pacheco said, "who think they can get rich in a day."

"Won't you look where Paz believed that the ghost pointed?" Señora Pacheco begged. "Something might be hidden there."

"I will look to satisfy myself, but I doubt that any Spanish ghost showed Paz where his money is buried!"

The señor went to the patio, and the señora followed him. Pancho ran into the shed for some tools. Paz sat down in the kitchen and folded her hands patiently, waiting for her master to find the riches in the well.

As Señor Pacheco was a teacher, he looked at the rock well and asked himself questions. Was the fortune concealed, where Paz had said, in the ground below the iron ring at the edge of the well? Did the sun not rise near this ring that stood in a line with the old tree? He frowned at himself for asking impertinent questions about the sun and the tree.

Although the señor had seen the old rock well hundreds of times, he examined it seriously now for its possibilities of

47

containing treasure. With his eyes he judged the well in the patio was four feet high. He put his hand on the rocks laid around the well and assumed they were a foot wide. The space between the rocks seemed too narrow to hold a treasure.

Señor Pacheco stared at the ground below the iron ring. He suspected there was some truth in what Paz had said because the treasure could be buried at the edge of the well. In his imagination he saw that some rock at the edge of the well might hide a cavity under the ground.

"Here, papa!" Pancho gave him a small mining pick.

"Bring me the rope ladder," his father said.

When Pancho brought him the ladder, he let himself down in the well since he knew that the water never rose above twelve feet. He peered around the well to see if he could detect any rock which might conceal a cavity. All the rocks were neatly plastered together and looked the same except one reddish orange stone. He realized this stone had some copper, which made its rare color, but it seemed larger than the others.

Señor Pacheco ran his fingers around the orange stone and it slipped. "Oh, Lord!" he exclaimed because this appeared to be in the ground below the iron ring. He slid out the rock and saw a leather cord which he jerked. A goat-skin sack, the size of a five-pound bag of sugar, fell on his hand. He opened the sack and it was full of gold coins.

As he went up the rope ladder, he said excitedly, "Here, here, son!" He gave Pancho the sack and climbed down the ladder.

"Heavens!" cried the señora when Pancho showed her the money.

Señor Pacheco pulled four more little sacks out of the cavity. All of them were filled with gold coins. The cavity was the length of his arm which he rolled back and forth to make

Señor Pacheco felt sorry for Paz as she wept over her father's grave

sure no more sacks were hidden. As he stepped out of the well, his señora was counting money.

She asked, "Didn't I tell you that the miserly Spaniard buried his fortune here? Now we can have a big house and fine clothes and even a carriage with good horses!"

Pancho touched his father's sleeve. "Now that you have money, will you buy me the paint-box from Europe?"

His father smiled. "Certainly, my son."

"I want to draw more mountains and paint them in beautiful colors for Paz!"

"Where is she?" the señor asked suddenly.

"I left her in the kitchen," Pancho answered.

They found Paz asleep with her hands folded in the lap of her old rose-colored skirt. The deep blue shawl had fallen on the floor, and her head was bobbing on her shoulder.

Pancho cried, "We found all the money in the well!"

Her almond eyes flew open. "I am happy for you!"

"My mountains aren't enough for Paz. She must have something else!"

"A black silk shawl," his mother added.

"No, no," Paz said humbly. She did not feel worthy of the black silk shawl any more than she had felt a right to the buried treasure. "Please give me only a wreath of flowers for my father's grave."

"You shall have many wreaths of flowers," the señor promised, "and I will go with you to the grave tomorrow."

Paz looked forward to the morrow when she could spread pretty wreaths of flowers on her father's grave. She would cover her face with both hands when she wept from her loss and the señor was sympathetic.

Pancho shouted, "Paz must have a black silk shawl and shoes!"

Paz glanced at her bare feet and smiled faintly. All of her life she had wanted a pair of shoes and now she could have them.

Pancho laughed. "We should call them 'the ghost's shoes!' "

THE DRUNKEN LIZARD

The drunken lizard

THE DRUNKEN LIZARD

I T WAS THE FIRST DAY of the term. Hundreds of boys were
in the patio of the school waiting for the bell to ring. An
old Spanish priest with gray whiskers named Padre Antonio
was pacing up and down the patio to make the boys keep
quiet. He walked with his hands in the pockets of his black
robe, and he had a grim expression on his face. His thin lips
were pressed into a line beneath his hawk nose and his eyes
were on the ground. When he raised his eyes, he saw a new
pupil standing apart from a crowd of small boys.

The new pupil thrust out his bottom lip and thought darkly:
Life in Mexico City was ugly . . . when he lived in Guanajuato
he had a big playroom . . . why did his family have to move
to Mexico City and take a little apartment that had no space
for a playroom where he could draw pictures of soldiers. . . .

A dark boy called Prieto went up to the new pupil and
asked, "Who are you?"

"My name is Francisco Pacheco," he said, "but most people
call me Pancho."

Prieto laughed as he looked Pancho up and down from his
head to his heels. He was taller than the other boys and had
a pot belly. "You have such a big stomach," said Prieto
bitingly, "that you should be called *Panzón!*"

Pancho winced. He was too big for his age and felt it
keenly.

55

Diego Rivera.

Padre Antonio

Prieto turned to the crowd of small boys and said in a low voice, "Let's name that strict old man with the big nose," he pointed at Padre Antonio who was watching some older boys, *"Padre Metiche!* Father Buttinski!"

All the boys shrieked, *"Metiche!"* and held their stomachs while they giggled louder and louder. Padre Antonio looked tall and thin in his black robe as he strode up to the crowd and demanded the reason for the noise.

Prieto drawled innocently, "We were only laughing at the word *metiche.*"

Padre Antonio narrowed his eyes and said sternly, "That is a bad word."

The boys hid their grins and poked one another because Padre Antonio did not suspect that Prieto had nicknamed him Father Buttinski. Pancho smiled but his stomach felt empty and griped from anxiety. Something was telling him that he would not be happy at this school. He put his hand in his pocket and squeezed a green clay frog which he carried for good luck.

The bell rang. Pancho lagged behind the other boys as they fell into lines and marched up the stairs. He wished that he could go home and draw until night came . . . his father said he was eight years old and must begin school now . . . but he did not want to learn how to read and write . . . he only wanted to stay at home and draw soldiers and paint beautiful flowers. . . .

All the boys sat down in a large room that had a picture on its wall of Don Porfirio Diaz, the President of Mexico. When a tall priest with a big stomach that bulged out of his robe walked into the room, the boys shouted, *"Buenos días,* Padre!" He smiled and said in Spanish, "If I were deaf, I could hear your good morning!" The boys laughed and snickered. They liked Padre Lucas, the principal of the school, because he joked with them.

Padre Lucas bowed his head, crossed himself, and began to pray in an eloquent voice. The boys prayed with him in low voices that sounded like the drone of hundreds of bees. Many boys raised their eyes and looked at the Padre while they prayed. His double chin was squashed on his chest, and his fat cheeks quivered as a stream of holy words rolled from his lips.

Pancho did not pray with the rest of the boys because his father was a freethinker who had brought him up without any beliefs. During the prayers his thoughts wandered back to what his father had said last night, "Please behave at school . . . the Padre taught me when I was a boy . . . we are still good friends . . . tomorrow night he will come to our house. . . ."

A little perspiration wet the Padre's dark broad forehead and made the spectacles over his shrewd gray eyes misty when he reached the end of the prayers. The bell rang while he said, *"En el nombre del Padre, del Hijo y del Espíritu Santo,* amen. . . ." All the boys marched out of the room to their classes. As Pancho followed the crowd of small boys, he longed to have Padre Lucas for his teacher instead of Padre Antonio.

That night Padre Lucas had a bottle of wine under his arm when he came to Pancho's house. His father poured out some wine for the Padre and gave Pancho a little. The wine tasted sweet and spread a warm glow through his pot belly. He wished that he could drink up all the wine in the bottle.

His father clinked his glass with the priest's and said, "Good health!"

Padre Lucas cried, "Good health! I am happy to be with you tonight."

Pancho stared at his father when he sipped his wine and said, "It made me sad to leave Guanajuato, but I did not earn sufficient money from teaching school. I had to come to Mexico City and work for the government."

Padre Lucas put his glass down and said, "Those Reform Laws are worrying me. Years ago, when the Laws were enforced, we priests hid our robes and our classes in religion so that the government would not suspect we ran a Catholic school. Since Don Porfirio Diaz has been the president of Mexico, we have worn our robes and taught religion openly. But today I heard that inspectors are being sent around to schools to see if they teach religion."

Pancho's father said, "Perhaps Don Porfirio Diaz is going to enforce the Reform Laws for a little while to calm down the liberals who are protesting against the influence of the Church on education. If the Laws are enforced, an inspector would fine your school for teaching religion."

The Padre said shrewdly, "When an inspector comes to our school, we could play a trick on him and make him think that we do not teach religion if we had a pupil who is not religious, like Pancho, to answer his questions."

Pancho interrupted, "I want to help you play a trick on an inspector. . . ."

A few days later Padre Lucas and a tall sallow-faced man walked into the large room where prayers were held. The Padre pointed to the picture of Don Porfirio Diaz and said, "Señor, you may see from it that our school is not religious. We do not hang pictures of the saints on our walls," he smiled, "but a portrait of the President of Mexico. Although the school is taught by priests, we keep our beliefs to ourselves.

If you care to ask one of our boys questions about religion, you will see that we do not teach religion."

Padre Lucas glanced at the roomful of boys and said in a loud voice, "Francisco Pacheco, please stand up."

When Pancho stood up, the inspector asked, "Do you believe in God?"

Pancho shook his head and said earnestly, "No, señor."

The inspector nodded approvingly.

Most of the boys stared angrily at Pancho because they were religious. When he saw the ugly looks on their faces, he knew they would try to hurt him. He clutched the green clay frog which had always brought him luck and thought: Maybe it could prevent those boys from doing something to him. . . .

The inspector continued, "Do you believe in the Church?"

"No, señor," Pancho said slowly, "I do not believe in the Church."

"I am satisfied," the inspector said. "I will say in my report that religion is not taught here." He walked out of the room with Padre Lucas.

The room was silent until the sound of the inspector's footsteps had faded away. Then Prieto pointed at Pancho and yelled, "He's an atheist!" Another boy shouted, "He committed the sin of blasphemy!" The cry, "He is a heretic!" spread from boy to boy. As the bell rang, Prieto screamed, "We should punish him!" Many boys in the school talked against Pancho Pacheco while they crowded out of the room and marched to their classes.

For days the boys in Pancho's class treated him as if he were an enemy. They stared coldly at him and threw spitballs at his back when Padre Antonio called on him to recite. During recess Prieto banded the boys together and made them stay away from Pancho. He whistled as loud as he could to show the boys that he did not care if they were unfriendly.

One day an older boy came up to him at recess and said, "Don't take it seriously because those little boys avoid you. I am not religious either."

He sat down beside Pancho and talked about himself. "When I grow up," he said, "I am going to be a painter."

Pancho kept silent. He never told any boy that he would rather paint flowers than play football because he was afraid of being called a sissy.

The boy said, "Next year I want to study at an art school."

"What is that?" Pancho asked quickly.

"That," the older boy replied and smiled at his childish ignorance, "is where you can learn how to paint."

When the bell rang, Pancho ran up to Prieto and the boys in his class. He was so excited that he did not see the mean expressions on their faces. His heart pounded while he wished that he could go to an art school and learn how to become a painter. He marched into the classroom and started to sit down at his desk when Prieto pulled away his chair. Pancho fell on the floor and let out a nasty word as he scrambled to his feet.

Padre Antonio came in the room and demanded, "What was that noise?"

Prieto said, "Please excuse me, Father, but I fell down."

"You are a dirty filthy liar!" Pancho screamed.

The Padre cried, "Where did you learn such bad words?" His gray whiskers quivered as he whirled around and grabbed a ruler off his desk. He strode up to Pancho and took hold of his collar. Pancho gnashed his teeth while Padre Antonio whipped his pants with the ruler until his behind stung.

Many boys nudged one another with their elbows and whispered, "He should be punished . . . the Padre is doing right to punish him. . . ."

Padre Antonio frowned at his class and said, "You may sit down, Francisco!"

Tears of anger came to Pancho's eyes. He put his head down to hide his tears and drew pictures of his father on the desk. His father, he thought, loved him even if Padre Antonio and those boys hated him. . . .

At the end of class he walked slowly out of the room behind the boys. They waited for him in the patio and knocked him to the ground. Four boys held his legs and arms down while Prieto sat on his belly and punched his face. A crowd watched and shouted, "The Padre did not beat him enough! Give him some blows on the head! Kill the atheist Pancho Pacheco!"

Some boy yelled, "Here comes the Padre!"

Prieto and the boys scattered in all directions. Padre Antonio's long black robe twisted around his legs as he halfway ran toward Pancho. He threw one look over his shoulder at the Padre and raced out of the patio. The face of Prieto swam before his eyes and the yell, "Kill Pancho Pacheco," rang in his ears while he ran down a quiet street which led to his house.

Blood trickled from his nose as he sank down on an old gray fountain in the patio of his apartment house. He wiped his nose on the sleeve of his brown coat and called Prieto every dirty name he learned from the servants who had worked for his family. When he said the last filthy word he knew, he picked the dry blood out of his nose and looked around him.

Easter lilies were growing around the fountain, and pink and red geraniums were climbing on the walls of the patio. He pushed out his bottom lip and drew the flowers on his spelling tablet while he talked to himself. "I," he said, "will paint these flowers in watercolor and make a beautiful world of flowers on paper . . . Prieto and those boys can not hurt me now. . . ."

That night he begged, "Papa, can I go to an art school?"

His father said, "You are too young. Besides, I want you to go to military school. I thought you wanted to go because you draw soldiers."

Pancho argued, "I draw soldiers because I want to be a painter."

"Let's wait until you are older," said his father, "before we decide."

When Pancho woke up in the morning, he did not feel like going to school. As he pulled on his high-topped shoes, he remembered last Sunday afternoon . . . his father took him on a streetcar to an Indian village called Xochimilco which meant Place of Flowers . . . they walked up a cobblestone road in the village and came to some water . . . his father bargained with an Indian for a ride in a canoe . . . and the Indian paddled them down long canals that wound around islands of red carnations, Easter lilies, and daisies. . . .

After breakfast Pancho walked down to the main plaza and climbed on a streetcar going to Xochimilco. He sat back in his seat and looked at the people on the streets while he rode out of Mexico City. When he reached the country, he saw a few Indian peasants moving slowly down the road. One poor Indian, who had a crate of squash roped on his back, was walking beside a burro loaded with chicken-cages. His wife pattered down the road behind him with a basket of carnations on her head and a baby strapped to her back.

The peasants were walking back to their village of Xochimilco, carrying the squash and carnations they had raised on land near the canals, because they could not sell them in Mexico City. When the streetcar rolled into the village, Pancho saw a peasant making water under a tree. As he climbed off the streetcar, he felt hungry and went in the market to buy some food. He forgot about food when an Indian cried at him, *"Jarabe de axolotes, niño?"*

Pancho looked at the Indian. He was wrapped up in a dark blue *sarape* which covered his body from his chin to his ankles. His round brown face was old, but he had no wrinkles nor any hair on his cheeks. He had pushed his sombrero down on his head to keep the air out of his ears while he sold remedies for colds and pains. His toes stuck out of his sandals, and the ground around his feet was littered with bunches of herbs, clay bottles, and bowls of berries. Dead water lizards were hanging on the wall behind him.

"What," Pancho asked the Indian, "are *axolotes?*"

The Indian showed his white teeth when he pointed at a water lizard and cried, "That is an *axolotl!*" It had a tail, four feet and a purplish brown skin. He waved his hand toward the canals in the village and said, "Those waters are full of *axolotes.*" As he poured out some brown sirup from a clay bottle into a wooden spoon, he said, "Please taste this cough sirup. I made it from a few dead water lizards, and I call it *jarabe de axolotes.*"

Pancho sipped the cough sirup. It had a queer flavor that was neither sweet nor bitter nor sour.

"Have you never heard," the Indian asked, "about the winged *axolotl?*"

Pancho shook his head.

"Anybody," said he, "who sees the winged *axolotl* will live forever."

Pancho cried, "Did *you* ever see the winged *axolotl?*"

The Indian sold cough sirup made from dead water lizards

The Indian shrugged his shoulders. "No, but I heard about it from an old herb vendor who has gone to the other world."

"Where does the winged *axolotl* live?" asked Pancho excitedly.

"It swims and flies through the ocean. . . ." He dropped his voice and repeated the great secret as it was told to him by the herb vendor. "Only one man in a million men recognizes the winged *axolotl* because its body is golden like the sun. Sailors from all over the world always think it is a strange image made by the shining of the sun upon the waters of the ocean."

Pancho's eyes became dreamy and his mind wandered away. All of a sudden a winged *axolotl* was flying around and around in his imagination. . . .

It had long golden wings that sprouted out from its ears . . . the wings flapped while it glided on the waves of the ocean past ships . . . if a sailor recognized the lizard and cried out that it was the winged *axolotl*, it winked its beady eyes mysteriously and gave him the power to live forever.

Pancho shifted his feet and thought: If he lived for hundreds of years, he could paint all the people and things in the world. . . . He shut his eyes a second and wished that he could see the golden winged *axolotl*.

The Indian shouted at a woman, *"Jarabe de axolotes!"*

Pancho turned away in disgust and grumbled, "If I drank *axolotl* sirup until my stomach burst, it would not give me the power to live forever. . . ."

He thought about the winged *axolotl* on his way to school the following morning. When he came to a grocery store, he stopped and looked at its shelves. They were full of wine bottles wrapped in red and green paper. He licked his lips and wished that he could drink all the wine in the bottles.

A drunken man he saw one time floated through his mind. The man rocked his head and rolled his eyes as though he were seeing things . . . maybe some day he, Pancho, could get drunk and see things, too . . . Church bells pealed nine o'clock. School, he mused gloomily, it was time for school. . . .

He slung his books over his shoulder and walked slowly down the street. One night his father had said to him, "Men forget everything in the world when they are drunk." He, Pancho, wanted to get drunk very, very soon . . . and forget that he was unhappy because Prieto and the other boys hated him.

When he reached the school, the patio was empty. He threw out his chest to show that he was not afraid and walked into the classroom. Padre Antonio's back was turned, and his chalk squeaked as he wrote a lesson on the blackboard. When Prieto saw Pancho, he drew a picture of a fat devil with horns and scrawled below it, *"Panzón* Pacheco." He passed the picture to a boy, and it went around the class until some boy slipped it into Pancho's hand.

Pancho tore up the devil because he was tired of being persecuted. To his mind he had a right to believe in nothing as much as the boys had a right to believe in God and the Church. He chewed his bottom lip and glowered at Prieto until the bell rang. When the boys marched out to the patio, he lunged at Prieto and knocked him down. Some little fellow became so excited that he yelled Padre Antonio's nickname, "Father Buttinski!"

It was not Padre Antonio but Padre Lucas who grabbed Pancho by the collar just as he gave Prieto a black eye. The boys waved their hands at Pancho and cried in shrill voices to Padre Lucas, "He's an atheist! You should punish him! He hates Prieto and tried to kill him!"

Padre Lucas said to the boys, "It is recess time. You may go play."

The crowd broke up. Padre Lucas was alone with Pancho when he asked, "What is the trouble?"

Pancho made a face and muttered, "All the boys hate me because of those answers I gave to the inspector."

"Oh! I thought they would understand you were trying to help me fool him." Padre Lucas stroked his jowls and murmured, "Boys are savages."

The Padre put on his hat and walked out of the patio with Pancho. "Go home now," he said, "and tomorrow morning I will help you to make friends with the boys. Meet me in the sacristy of the Church of Jesus."

When morning came Pancho hurried to the sacristy. Padre Lucas patted his shoulder and said, "I am going to tell the boys that you did the school a great favor by giving those answers to the inspector."

Pancho grinned at the Padre.

"Wait for me until Mass is over," he said, "and I will bring some of the boys here to make friends with you."

Bells rang for church and Padre Lucas went to Mass. Pancho looked curiously around him at the sacristy. His eyes fell on a cross above a chest of drawers and two bottles of holy wine. He seized one of them and thought: At last his chance had come to drink all the wine he wanted . . . now he could get drunk and see things. . . . He threw back his head and drank.

Church bells rang as he finished the second bottle of wine. Padre Lucas and a crowd of boys flocked into the sacristy. Pancho's head was spinning and the smiles on the faces of Prieto and the other boys seemed to be hundreds of miles away. His ears felt numb when Padre Lucas tweaked them

Pancho drank the holy wine in the sacristy

and cried, "You are drunk!" The Padre chuckled. "You may go home. . . ."

The ground rocked under Pancho's feet as he left the sacristy and staggered down the street. He said to himself, "It is an earthquake. . . ." He waved his arms to keep the earth from knocking him down while he walked to the plaza where he saw four streetcars, piled one on top of the other, going to Xochimilco. As he went up to the bottom one, the steps moved up and down and almost tripped him, but he put his feet on them and climbed on board.

He sat back in his seat and closed his eyes while the streetcar whirled around and around Mexico City like a merry-go-round and made him feel dizzy. When he opened his eyes, he saw a burro riding down the road to Xochimilco on an Indian peasant. All of a sudden the peasant jumped up, with a big basket of Easter lilies on his back, and sat down on the burro. Pancho felt so happy when another peasant trotted down the road, driving along a herd of pigs, that the squealing of the pigs sounded like music to his ears.

A woman piped in his ears, *"Vamos a llegar!"* as the streetcar rolled into Xochimilco. Waves of heat were pouring through his body and rising to his head when he climbed off the streetcar. The sun glared on him and scorched his cheeks while he lurched down a cobblestone road that led to the canals. His throat burned and he mumbled, "Water . . . water. . . ." Canoes, Indian boatmen, and an island of lilies swirled before him as he stripped off his clothes and jumped into a canal to put out the fire in his body.

Minnows and fish grazed his legs while a purplish brown *axolotl* swam up to his elbow. Its body shimmered in the sun and two sunbeams were dancing on its head. When he saw a pair of long golden wings sprout out from its ears, he

Pancho was so drunk from the holy wine that he saw the winged *axolotl* who gave him the power to live forever and paint everything in the world

screamed, "You are not the sun but the winged *axolotl!*" Pancho burst out laughing when the *axolotl* winked its black eyes mysteriously. He did not know that a drunken lizard gave him the power to live forever.

MERCHANT OF ART

MERCHANT OF ART

I T WOULD HAVE BEEN easy for any thief to rob the old man
who sold peanuts on a little table near the school of art.
The old man was sick and some doctor had cut off his right
leg after a horse broke loose from a carriage and ran over
him. A carpenter made him a crude peg-leg which he could
strap to his stump, and he hobbled around on it while he
waited upon the boys who studied in the art school. Many
boys called the old man *El Pollo* because he looked as sad
as a half-starved chicken.

He drooped his head when he stood on the sidewalk beside
his little table with a sombrero pushed over his forehead to
shade his watery eyes from the sun. His brown face was lean
and bony and a few long black hairs grew on his chin. He
wore a pair of torn white trousers day in and day out with
the left leg down and the other leg doubled up under his peg.
The only shoe that he owned had a hole in the toe, and it was
on his foot.

A mongrel dog slept beside the old man when he played a
guitar and sang in a high voice to get people, who walked up
and down the street, to buy a ballad or two. The ballads were
printed on pink and yellow papers, and they lay on the ground
around his table with rocks over them to keep the wind from
blowing them away. Whenever he sold a ballad or some pea-

nuts, he put the money in a straw bag which he carried on the hip of his peg-leg.

Since the old man had never been robbed, he felt that his money was safe until one evening in the year 1898 when a policeman with a crooked nose and a long black mustache came up to him. The policeman had pulled his kepi down on his head, and his eyes were bloodshot. He wore a dark blue uniform trimmed with red, and a pistol and a club hung from his belt.

"Viejo," he said, "old man, I am going to take you to jail, unless you give me some money, because you do not have a license for your stall."

El Pollo argued, "I do not have a stall. All I have is this little table which I carry away with me every night when I go home to sleep."

The policeman fingered his club and looked menacingly at the old man.

"How much do you want?" he asked.

"Ten pesos," the policeman bullied.

The old man cried, "That is all I can make in a week!" He trembled as he emptied his straw bag on the table. There were eight pesos in the bag.

The policeman put the money in his pocket and walked across the street to a blue adobe saloon called The Gold Barrel. He met another policeman, who had a sallow face and a hairy mole on his cheek, at the saloon door. When the old man saw the policemen look at him and laugh, he thought angrily: They are friends . . . one of them took my money today . . . who knows if the other will rob me tomorrow . . . because they want money to get drunk. . . .

El Pollo shook his fist at the policemen while he watched them go into the saloon. He turned his head when a carriage rolled down the street and stopped in front of the art school. A tall, plump gentleman, wearing a round black hat and a short black cape around his shoulders, stepped out of the carriage. *El Pollo* looked at the gentleman but did not know who he was. His head drooped as he sat down beside his table and counted his peanuts.

A crowd of boys were standing in the patio of the school, and they said good evening to the gentleman when he walked up to them with a paint-box in his hand. He was Don Hugo Mengano, a painter who had become famous during the regime of Porfirio Diaz, the Dictator of Mexico. All the rich society people asked Don Hugo Mengano to paint their portraits because he was in style. He had just returned from Paris, where he spent the summer, and the boys had seen a picture of him in the newspaper only that morning.

Don Hugo Mengano nodded to the boys and left his hat and cape with the concierge before he went into the room where he would teach painting twice a week. It was a large room crowded with sixteen-year-old boys and two girls dressed in black who sat by themselves because not many women studied at the art school. The boys stopped talking when Don Hugo Mengano sat down and began to read the names of the students in his class off a sheet of paper.

When he came to the name of Francisco Pacheco, a fat boy with a pug nose raised his right arm and said, "I am here, Master!" Pancho was only twelve, but he had begged his father to let him study painting at night.

A boy who sat next to Pancho stood up as the Master said, "Julio Talavera," the last name on the list.

There was no class that night because the Master talked about his voyage to France. Pancho stared at his clothes while he paced up and down the room. He wore a fancy coat buttoned down the front and a black bow under his chin. His hair was long and his mustache had been trimmed to go with his Vandyke beard. He spoke with many flourishes of his hands while he described his visits to art galleries in Paris. "In a few words," he said in Spanish, "my journey showed me that we are living in an age in which the decent people of Mexico must look to France for culture."

The boys shook their heads and the girls nodded because they knew that all the rich people in Mexico were making voyages to France for culture, talking French, dressing in French costumes, and buying French paintings.

Don Hugo Mengano began to mix in French words with his Spanish, as though he wanted to show off, while he said, "I believe that every young Mexican artist should go to France and learn how to paint in the French manner. When the young artist returns home, he will find many things in Mexico that will inspire him to paint them. I, for example, have always found it an inspiration to do the portraits of the most distinguished persons in our society. While I was in Paris, I painted three charming daughters of a general of Don Porfirio Diaz who were sojourning abroad."

The bell rang. As Pancho walked out of the room behind some boys, he wished that he had the money to study painting in France. When he reached the sidewalk, he saw the old man playing his guitar in the light of a candle that was flickering on his table. A servant with a market basket in her hand, an Indian peasant carrying a small goat under his arm, and a carpenter with a table roped to his back had gathered on the sidewalk to hear the old man. Pancho lingered beside them and listened to the music.

El Pollo twanged his guitar and picked up a few pink and yellow papers strewn on the ground around his table. "Buy some ballads!" he cried shrilly. "For your money you get the words of ballads and pictures. . . ." He held the ballads up in the air to let the crowd see the pictures on them.

Pancho stared at a picture of some poor women with hungry faces who were holding empty baskets in their hands because they could not get any food. The servant laughed when she saw a picture of a peon, carrying a jug of water on his back, making love to a servant girl. She took a few centavos out of her bosom to buy that ballad while the Indian peasant, who had the goat under his arm, looked at a sad picture of an Indian family wandering in search of a home with their straw mats rolled over their shoulders.

The carpenter said out loud, "I like the pictures on the ballads!"

El Pollo said, "Yesterday I sold some peanuts to the man who makes these pictures. His name is José Guadalupe Posada and he works over there. . . ." He pointed his arm at a little workshop around the corner.

When Pancho heard the old man, he walked around the corner out of curiosity. A light was burning in the workshop and he stepped inside the door. He saw a heavy-set man, sitting on a stool, with his back hunched over a table. His dark brown face was bent over a picture that he was drawing. The curled ends of his black mustache hung down as though he had been drawing for hours. He had taken off his coat, and he was working in his vest. His pants had slipped up and the tops of his shoes were showing.

Pancho said, "Good evening, Señor Posada."

He looked up and asked, "Who are you?"

"I am studying to be a painter at the school of art."

"And what did you learn today, little man?"

Pancho said excitedly, "Many things, Señor Posada! One

of my painting masters has just come back from Paris. He told me and the boys in my class that we should go to France and learn how to paint like the French."

"All of that is nonsense!" Posada said. "Why should we paint like Frenchmen when we are Mexicans? I, for example, want to draw pictures of my own people ... the Indian peasants and the men who work on the streets and the servants who work in the houses of the rich. . . ."

"But what about the decent people?"

Posada laughed and asked, "You mean the few people in our country who say they are decent because they have money? When I draw those people, I like to ridicule them. They dress up in clothes from Paris and try to talk French and stuff their bellies at banquets and make politics and dance. . . ."

Pancho stared at him and thought: He is making fun of the rich people ... and he is right ... they are not decent because they have money. . . .

"The decent people," said Posada, "do not think I am an artist or even know I am alive. They never look at my pictures because they think that ballads are meant for their servants. But I do not care what those people think! I feel as if I were a great artist because all the poor people like to look at my pictures when they hear ballads sung on the streets."

"I believe you," said Pancho, "because I saw a crowd of poor people admiring your pictures on the way over here. I want to talk to you more, but it is getting late. Tomorrow evening I will come to see you again."

Pancho shook Posada's hand and walked out of the workshop, thinking: That man is as nice and simple as any man who works in a store ... but he speaks of himself as if he were a great artist ... maybe he is one because he draws

Indian peasants, servants, and peons who seem as alive as those on the streets . . . I wish that I could draw Indian men and women like he does . . . I think I will go to a market and draw some Indians tomorrow after school. . . ."

Early in the afternoon Pancho went to a market and drew three Indian peasant women who were selling clay jars, cabbages, and pigs. He finished the sketch toward evening and sauntered to the workshop. As he came in the door, he saw Posada standing beside the policeman who had a sallow face and a hairy mole on his cheek. The policeman was holding a ballad in his left hand and pointing to a picture on it of a soldier hanging from a tree.

"You drew this soldier," he said to Posada, "because you want to show people that soldiers are hanged when they run away from the army of Don Porfirio Diaz. I will go to the authorities and tell them that you are attacking Don Porfirio Diaz in this picture unless you give me some money."

Posada said angrily, "You do not care whether I attack Don Porfirio Diaz or not as long as I give you money!"

The policeman said, "I am going to take you to jail!"

Pancho screamed, "You can not take him to jail for drawing a soldier!"

Posada said calmly, "I will only go to jail for a day or two, little man. That is better than to pay a bribe!"

The policeman grabbed Posada by the arm and pushed Pancho out of the workshop. He muttered, *"Ese perro . . . that dog. . . "* as he watched the policeman lead Posada up the street to the city jail. When he could see them no longer, he walked around the corner. The old man saw Pancho go past him with his bottom lip thrust out angrily and an ugly look on his face.

Pancho was thinking: They say that the jail is full of bed-

81

Posada in jail

bugs and fleas . . . and prisoners are only given hard bread to eat. . . . He hurried into a dark little store and bought some buns. Holding the bread in his hand, he strode up the street to the jail. As he wandered through it, looking for Posada, a drunken prisoner whistled and shouted dirty words at him.

Posada was pacing up and down a cell with his belly out and his hands clasped behind him. He had pushed his hat back on his head, and he was frowning. When Pancho slipped the buns through the bars, he said, "Many thanks for the favor that you did me!" He stuffed the buns in his coat pocket to save them until he became hungry. "That policeman," he said furiously, "was no better than a thief! He tried to get a bribe from me!"

Pancho asked, "Were you really attacking Don Porfirio Diaz when you drew the picture of the soldier?"

"I felt sorry," said Posada, "for that soldier and all the soldiers who have been hanged or shot for trying to run away from his army."

"I saw Don Porfirio Diaz one time," said Pancho. "He was dressed up in a beautiful uniform with medals on his chest and a plumed hat and a sword. He looked nice, but he must be a bad man."

"He is," said Posada, "because he has kept himself in power so long. He has been our president for twenty-two years, and he has ruled us like a dictator. He let a few people get rich, but he oppresses the rest of the people in our country. Even the policemen, who work for him on the streets, earn barely enough money to buy their beans. The policemen are so poor that they have become mean. They will do anything to get money."

"Now I understand," said Pancho.

"But do not worry about the policemen, little man. They

will not bother you if you have no money. Go on painting. . . ."

Pancho stayed at home the following afternoon and painted the Indian women he had sketched in the market. When night fell, he walked slowly to the school of art. He did not realize how late it was until he stepped into Don Hugo Mengano's room. The bell had rung and a few boys, who admired the Master, had lingered after class to talk to him. Pancho nodded to Julio Talavera, the boy who sat beside him, as he went up to the crowd around the Master.

"I told you," the Master was saying, "that I painted three daughters of a general of Don Porfirio Diaz while I was in Paris. The young ladies are as beautiful as they are wealthy, and I painted them in lovely gowns which a French modiste designed. They were charmed with the portrait when it was finished and they told me," the Master smiled, "that I am a great painter."

Pancho stared at Don Hugo Mengano and thought: That man is not a great painter . . . but the daughters of the general and the other rich people around Don Porfirio Diaz think that he is a great painter . . . because he dresses up in a fancy costume . . . and he makes stylish portraits of them. . . .

The Master said, "No one has seen the portrait in Mexico, and it will be unveiled at my home on Saturday afternoon at five o'clock. I invited all the decent people to the unveiling, and I hope that you boys will come."

Julio said, "I will come with pleasure, Master!"

The other boys said, "Thank you, Master!"

Don Hugo Mengano smiled at them and said, "Until Saturday. . . ."

All the boys crowded out of the room behind the Master. Pancho and Julio began to talk as they left the school and

Pancho and Julio stopped to buy some peanuts from the old man who was
singing a ballad

strolled down the sidewalk. The old man was standing beside his little table, strumming his guitar and singing, with his mongrel dog asleep at his foot. A ragged boy, holding a pile of newspapers under his arm, was listening to him. Pancho and Julio stopped to buy some peanuts. When the old man turned around to wait on them, the sallow-faced policeman walked out of The Gold Barrel.

The policeman fingered the hairy mole on his cheek as he came up to the old man and took him aside. He said in a low voice, "If you want to sell things here on the sidewalk, you must give me some money."

El Pollo cried, "No, I gave your friend one bribe! This is enough!"

Pancho said to the policeman, "You took Posada to jail because he would not give you any money! Now you are trying to bribe the old man!"

The policeman looked at Pancho and said, "Keep your nose out of this!"

No thief had ever robbed the old man, but the policeman grabbed the straw bag off the hip of his peg-leg. There were only a few pesos in it because the old man had a bad week. He hobbled around the policeman as fast as he could and tried to grab the bag, for he needed his money to buy tortillas and beans. When he snatched the bag away, the policeman slipped out his club and hit the old man on the head. He was killed by the blow instantly, and blood poured from his nose as he fell to the sidewalk.

Pancho threw a rock at the policeman and yelled, "Murderer!" The policeman stuffed the bag in his pocket and started to run away when the old man's dog jumped on him and bit his leg. Julio and the ragged newsboy picked up some dirt and rocks and slung them at the policeman. He pulled out his pistol and shot the dog because it would not let go of his leg.

The policeman with the crooked nose and the long black mustache ran out of The Gold Barrel when he heard the shot. People began to gather on the sidewalk. They stared at the pools of blood around the old man and the dog and mumbled, "Somebody killed them . . . there is a crime here. . . ."

Julio yelled at the sallow-faced policeman, "I saw you rob the old man!"

The other policeman gave Julio a slap on the jaw which knocked him down. "That," he said, "will teach you that policemen do not rob people!"

The sallow-faced policeman yelled, "The old man tried to rob me and I killed him in self-defense! Then his dog went mad and bit me!" He raised his pants and showed the crowd the red marks of the dog's teeth in his leg.

"You are a thief and a murderer!" Pancho shouted.

The policeman with the crooked nose waved his club at Pancho and the crowd and said, "Get away before I take all of you to jail!"

The people were afraid of the policemen and scattered.

As Julio walked away with Pancho, he said, "Poor old man. . . ."

Pancho cried, "Don Porfirio Diaz is to blame for this! He rules us with his sword like a dictator! And he gives his policemen clubs and pistols and the power over us! We can not do anything to them when they rob and kill people because Don Porfirio Diaz does not pay them enough!"

Julio rubbed his sore jaw and said, "I hope that my face does not look too bad to go to the Master's house on Saturday afternoon."

Pancho blurted out, "The Master is no better than those policemen!"

Julio said, "The Master has nothing to do with those policemen!"

"They are all the same thing!" Pancho cried. "The policemen work for Don Porfirio Diaz, and the Master lives off of the rich people around Don Porfirio Diaz! He only paints the rich people, and they must give him a lot of money for his portraits! He sells his art like a merchant. . . ."

"I do not care what you think!" said Julio. "I am going to the Master's house on Saturday afternoon to see his painting unveiled."

Pancho thought angrily: I can not do anything to Don Porfirio Diaz nor the policemen . . . but I can do something to the Master . . . I will make him ridiculous and discredit him before all the rich people who think he is such a great painter . . . when they come to see his painting unveiled. . . .

Early Saturday afternoon Pancho walked to Don Hugo Mengano's home with his painting of the Indian women rolled under his arm. When he knocked on the door of the house, a servant girl asked what he wished.

"I have come," he said, "to see the Master's painting unveiled."

"You came very early," she said, "because the painting will not be unveiled for an hour or more. But you may come inside and wait."

She led Pancho into a long drawing room furnished with gilt chairs, mirrors, and gold brocade sofas. He saw the Master's painting, standing on an easel at the head of the room, covered with a pale blue curtain. When the servant left him alone, he pushed the curtain back and tacked his painting on the Master's. Then he slid the curtain over his painting.

He sat and watched all the rich people drive up to Don Hugo Mengano's house in fine carriages. Thin and stout gentlemen wearing frock coats and top hats stepped out of carriages and gave their hands to old ladies in long black dresses, with black shawls wrapped around their heads, or young ladies in stylish Parisian gowns. Two fat generals with jowls and shiny medals on their chests strutted up to the house because they had been sent by Don Porfirio Diaz to represent him at the unveiling of the painting.

The Master stood at the door of the drawing-room and greeted all the decent people as they crowded up to him, talking in French and Spanish. A few art students, a poet with long hair and an art critic wearing a monocle over his right eye followed the crowd into the room. As Julio sat down, he nodded at Pancho who was sitting on a gilt chair in front of the easel. The Master shook hands with a pompous gentleman who arrived last. He was the director of a newspaper, and he had brought a photographer with him.

All the decent people clapped when Don Hugo Mengano walked up to his painting. A boy, dressed in the uniform of a page, was standing beside the easel. The Master bowed and said, "I am sorry that the daughters of the general are not here this afternoon to see the unveiling of their portrait, but I am sure that you will recognize them as they are distinguished members of our society." He gestured at the boy to pull back the curtain.

Astonished cries rose from the people when they saw a painting of three Indian peasants instead of three society ladies. One of the peasants was sitting on her knees beside a basket of cabbages with a dark blue shawl wrapped around her head and shoulders. Another peasant was holding a little pig in her arms and looking down at a few pigs huddled near her long pink skirt. The other woman was squatting on the ground, with some clay pots and jars piled around her bare feet, and combing her long black hair.

The director of the newspaper said in a loud voice, "The Master has deceived us! He told us that he painted three daughters of a general, and he has painted three Indian women!"

A society lady held a bottle of smelling salts up to her nose and whispered, "*Quelle horreur. . . .*" Another lady whisked a lace handkerchief before her face and said under her breath "*Qué escándalo. . . .*"

Don Hugo Mengano's face was very pale and he cried, "Someone played a trick on me!" His former admirers would not listen to his protests, and they began to attack the painting. Pancho laughed because he had discredited the Master before all the rich people who thought he was so great.

Some portly gentleman waved his fat hands at the painting and cried, "It is scandalous!" His fleshy cheeks quivered as he burst into a tirade of abuse against the painting. "The Master has painted three Indian women from the market in their most vulgar poses. Selling cabbages, holding a pig, and even—" he exploded, "combing her hair to pick out the lice!"

The art critic looked at the painting through his monocle, turned up his nose, and said, "I believe that painting belongs in a servant's room!"

Pancho became furious while he listened to the criticism of his painting. He stood up and shouted at the rich people, "You are snobs! Stupid snobs! You are criticizing me because I painted some poor Indians!"

All the decent people closed their mouths and stared at him.

One society lady peered at Pancho through her opera glasses and asked out loud, "Has the boy gone mad?"

The Master said, "He must be mad because he came in here and tacked his painting over mine!" He tore the painting of the Indians off the easel.

Everybody looked at his painting. The general's daughters were sitting on a gold couch, and they wore long white dresses. Their dark hair fell to their shoulders, and they had crowns of white flowers on their heads.

The society ladies sighed and murmured, *"C'est très beau. . . ."*

Many gentlemen shook their heads and cried, *"Es muy elegante!"*

The director of the newspaper gave Don Hugo Mengano an embrace and said in Spanish, "Congratulations! It is a great painting!"

Pancho yelled, "Idiots! The Master is a bad painter, but José Guadalupe Posada is a great artist!"

The ladies and gentlemen nudged one another with their elbows and whispered, "Who is Posada?" because they had never heard of him. And none of those persons, who were so fashionable in 1898, ever dreamed that some day Don Hugo Mengano and his portraits might be forgotten while this Posada, a man whom they did not know existed, would be recognized as a great artist because he drew all the poor people and even the rich people of Mexico.

The poet with the long hair said, "Oh, the boy is talking about some man called Posada who does engravings for ballads that cost a few centavos!"

All the decent people turned their backs on Pancho and praised the painting of the general's daughters. Little girls laid baskets of roses beside the painting, and the photographer took a picture of it for his newspaper. Young and old ladies crowded around Don Hugo Mengano to congratulate him. Pancho ran out of the drawing-room when the Master kissed a lady's hand and said, "Yes, madam, I am still the great Don Hugo!"

DISCOVERY

DISCOVERY

O LD AGUIRRE walked slowly around the room while the boys in his class sketched a naked Mexican woman who sat on a small platform. She did not move her head, and her brown body was as motionless as a statue. The scratch of pencils, a few whispers, and the occasional sound of a carriage rolling down the street were the only noises that could be heard in the classroom.

It was Old Aguirre's last class for the night in the school of art. He looked dignified, walking up and down the room, with his white head in the air. His clothes were fashioned after the gentlemen who lived in Paris. He wore a black coat with long lapels, a high-necked vest, and black trousers. His white collar shone, and a pearl was pinned in his dark cravat.

All of a sudden Old Aguirre stopped beside a fat boy whose trousers were wrinkled and soiled. The boy had taken off one of his shoes and undone his tie so that he could draw in comfort. His dark hair was tangled over his forehead, and his pop eyes were darting from the Mexican woman to his paper.

Old Aguirre peered over the boy's shoulder.

A stubby pencil was gripped between the boy's long broad fingers. His nails were smudged with lead and his knuckles jutted out while he drew the Mexican woman laboriously. She was the first nude woman he had ever drawn.

Old Aguirre said very slowly, "I like your sketch."

The whole class looked up at Old Aguirre because it was not his custom to admire drawings. Night after night he pointed out the errors that boys made in their sketches. They listened to his criticism with much respect, for he was not only a drawing master but the esteemed old director of the school of art who had celebrated his seventy-fifth birthday that summer.

He put his wrinkled hand on the boy's shoulder and said, "It is good, Pacheco. You show imagination in your sketch of the model. . . ." The director glanced at the Mexican woman. "But you lack technique here and there. . . ."

The bell rang as he said, "I would like to talk to you, Pacheco. Why don't you come to my studio tomorrow evening?"

Surprised whispers spread from boy to boy. The old director seldom invited any of the students to his studio because he led a retired life.

Old Aguirre picked up his hat and walked out of the room. All the boys pushed and shoved one another as they crowded around Pancho Pacheco. They stepped on his feet and jabbed him in the back while they tried to see the sketch on the arm of his chair. Everybody wanted to know what there was so wonderful about the sketch that had made Old Aguirre invite him to his den.

A boy called Pepe was jealous of the drawing and said, "Our director must be going crazy in his old age if he thinks this is any good!"

The crowd turned away from Pancho Pacheco and looked at Pepe. A few boys shouted angrily at him, "Old Aguirre will never go crazy! He is one of the best painters in Mexico! We are lucky to have him for a director!"

Pancho Pacheco pulled on the shoe, which he had taken off so that he could draw in comfort, while the boys quarreled with Pepe.

A fellow saw him put on his shoe and roared, "Pancho's feet smell!"

The crowd turned around and watched Pancho tie up his shoe-laces. No one said a word for a minute or two, but several boys frowned and had sullen faces because Old Aguirre had invited Pancho instead of them to his studio.

A boy sneered, "Pancho has a hole in his pants. . . ."

"Pancho's lunch is on his shirt!" cried another boy.

Somebody yelled, "Pancho takes a bath once a month!"

Pancho laughed. He did not care how he looked.

Pepe grabbed the sketch, waved it in the air and jeered, "The only thing that Pancho drew in his sketch were the buttocks of the model!"

All the boys rushed toward Pepe and pressed close to him while they craned their necks over his shoulder and looked down at the sketch.

One boy joked, "Yes, Pancho drew the model's buttocks more than any other part of her body! He really attacked the model from her tail-end!"

The boys hee-hawed. They were older than Pancho and taunted him by crying, "Pancho is a baby! He never drew a woman's behind until today!"

Pancho's cheeks burned the color of a sausage. He snatched the drawing away from Pepe and held it above his head as he poked his way through the crowd. When he reached the door, he faced the boys and snorted, "I might be a baby, but I can draw a woman's hind much better than you boys can!"

Pepe lunged at him to pull his hair, but he ran out of the room.

It was a summer night in Mexico City and rain had begun to fall. The drizzle cooled his flushed cheeks while he thought: I, Pancho Pacheco, do not care what those boys say about me . . . only one thing matters to me . . . I must learn how to draw women's bodies . . . because Aguirre said I lack technique.

As Pancho walked down the street, he picked his nose and pondered: Old Aguirre's model is not enough . . . I need a model for myself so that I can sketch her hundreds of times . . . then I will learn how to draw women from their necks to their hinds . . . but I do not have the money to pay a model.

When he was nearly home, he stopped and meditated: If I gave some candy to Juana, maybe she would pose for me. . . . Pancho glanced at a grocery store across the street called La Madrid. He said to himself: I hate the man who owns that store . . . he is a Spaniard named Don Tomás who always cheats me . . . but it is the only place where I can buy some candy for Juana.

Pancho stood under a street-lamp and counted the money in his pocket. He had seventy centavos and went into La Madrid with the money in his hand.

When Don Tomás saw Pancho, he squinted his miserly eyes.

Pancho looked at the candy in all the boxes and tried to pick out a good kind that might tempt Juana. His eyes fell on a jar of cherries.

"I want," he pointed to the cherries, "one hundred grams of those."

Don Tomás said, "One hundred grams of cherries will cost ninety centavos."

Pancho argued, "The sign on the jar says they cost seventy centavos!"

"It is an old sign." Don Tomás twitched his mouth. "Prices

have gone up! If you want the cherries, they will cost you ninety centavos."

"Give them to me!" Pancho cried impatiently.

Don Tomás laid the bag of cherries on the counter. Pancho flung the seventy centavos down, snatched the bag and raced out of the store.

Just as he reached the sidewalk, Don Tomás ran to the door and yelled, "You cheated me out of twenty centavos! Stop!"

Pancho sped up the street. His fat legs went faster and faster while he thought: Why should I stop . . . I did not cheat Don Tomás out of twenty centavos . . . that *gachupin* . . . dirty Spaniard tried to overcharge me twenty centavos.

Don Tomás yelled no more.

Pancho slowed down his pace and ambled home. He clutched the bag of cherries as he climbed up a stairway that led to the roof of his apartment house. It was a large flat roof which held several water closets with bad smells and a row of small rooms where the servants lived. He rapped on the door of the young Indian girl who helped his mother in the kitchen.

"Juana. . . ." He whispered the girl's name.

She opened the door and cried, "Don Pancho!"

He strode into her room. A candle was flickering before a picture of the Virgin of Guadalupe which hung on the wall. Two old gingham skirts, a blouse, and a black shawl dangled from rusty nails. A faded blue and red cotton blanket, which Juana had woven, was folded on her straw mat.

Pancho undid the bag so that Juana could see the cherries. "I will give you these," he said, "if you let me draw you without any clothes."

Juana was shocked and covered her face with her hands. Her black hair was parted in the middle and fell in two

Diego Rivera.

**Juana had jet black eyes and black hair that fell in two braids down
her back**

braids down her back. Only the part of her hair showed as she spoke to him through the palms of her hands. "My godmother," she mumbled, "brought me from my village to work in your father's house. She would feel disgraced if you drew me in my flesh. . . ."

"Your godmother would never find out!" Pancho cried. He pictured the godmother in his imagination, for he had seen her many times. Her face was as shriveled as old brown leather, and her body had shrunken from age. She always wore a long black dress and wrapped a black shawl around her head.

"My godmother," Juana murmured, "will come to see your father in the autumn. She waits until the year is almost over to pay her respects to him because she was his nurse when he was a boy. If your father learns that you drew me in my bare flesh and tells my godmother, she will disown me."

Pancho looked at her with pity because the only person she had on earth was an old godmother. "My father," he cried impulsively, "lets me do whatever I want! He would not care if I drew you."

Juana stared at him. Her nose and chin were shaped as fine as if they had been carved from stone. "Do you speak the truth?" she asked fearfully.

Pancho saw the fear in her jet black eyes and teased, "Silly girl! You are fifteen years old, but you are as afraid as if you were a child."

The high cheekbones of her long thin face became crimson.

He was fourteen but felt older than she. "Don't you know that I," he asked arrogantly, "am going to be a painter and will paint hundreds of women someday?"

She tightened her deep red lips in a severe line.

He took a tiny cherry out of the bag and gave it to Juana to tempt her.

It was the first cherry she had ever eaten and she licked her mouth.

"Take them all," he gave her the bag, "and undress so I can draw you."

She put her hand in her bosom and pulled out a knotted rag in which she carried money. The rag was empty and she tied the cherries up in it. She turned her back on him while she slipped off her old yellow blouse and long full pink skirt that was faded from washing and had a blue gingham patch.

"Sit down on it," he pointed to the straw mat on which she slept, "and raise your chin so that I can draw you from your neck to your bottom!"

She sat on her mat and looked up at the ceiling. Her two braids came unfastened and hair streamed around her hips. Pancho did not glance at her hair nor her face while he sketched the difficult lines of her body.

He drew one sketch of her slowly and painstakingly. He could have drawn her all night, but she stopped him when church bells pealed midnight. "Don Pancho," she asked quietly, "don't you think it is time to rest?" She covered herself with her black shawl and waited for him to leave the room.

When morning came he took the sketch with him to breakfast. He was the first one at the table and spread the drawing of Juana's body over his plates. As he studied it, he knitted his brows and thought uneasily: I feel that the lines of her body are better than the nude I drew in Old Aguirre's class, but I am not sure. . . .

His mother came to the table with a soupbowl full of boiled rice and milk. She was about to set the bowl down before him when her eyes fell on the drawing. *"Ay, Jesus!"* she cried and dropped the bowl.

Big pools of milk swam on the paper and flooded it. Tears welled in Pancho's eyes while he stared at the ruins of his art. Kernels of rice were floating in the milk and trickling down the body of Juana. He bit his lips to keep from crying and sponged off the milk with the tablecloth. As he laid the sketch in the sun to dry, he mourned: I would not have cared if she had ruined my shirt or shoes. . . .

His mother's sharp voice pierced his ears. "It is immoral," she scolded, "to draw naked women!"

Pancho cried, "I must learn how to draw them if I am going to be a painter!" He made a face at his mother because she was so old-fashioned.

His father came into the room.

Pancho loved his father more than his mother and shouted, "Mama ruined it!" He pointed to the sketch.

"It deserved no better fate," she said wryly.

His father bent over the wet sketch and looked closely at it, for he had always sympathized with his son's desire to be a painter. "It seems to me," he murmured, "that Pancho is drawing nude women now so that he will be able to paint them later on."

"I have no sympathy," his mother said, "with Pancho's ambition to become a painter if he intends to paint naked women. That is sinful!"

"Let us have peace," his father said, "while we eat."

A heavy silence fell over the table. Pancho frowned at his mother and asked himself: Why can't she understand . . . women's bodies mean nothing to me except to put on paper . . . but I do not care what she says . . . I will draw Juana every night until I can draw the lines of her body skillfully.

His face was dark and gloomy when he left home. He pulled his hat over his eyes and walked slowly down the street while he thought: My mother spilled the bowl of rice on purpose because she wanted to ruin my sketch. . . .

He did not see a hole in the street and twisted his ankle so hard that he grimaced from pain. As he rubbed his sore ankle, he became crosser and crosser. He grumbled: I do not feel like going to high school . . . all of my classes bore me . . . I wish it were night so that I could go to art school. . . .

It was a miserable day.

He went to Old Aguirre's studio in the evening. The old man leaned back in his armchair and said, "I invited you to come here . . ."

Pancho glanced around him at the studio. Paintings of old masters hung on the walls. A mahogany table and a few black leather armchairs were in the room. Some bookcases, full of books about art, stood near a window.

"Because I was curious. . . ." A light came into his aged brown eyes. "You seem to have much talent and I wanted to talk to you. Hmm, do you intend to graduate from the school and teach art later?"

"To graduate, yes. But I do not want to teach." Pancho looked Old Aguirre in the eyes. "I want to be a painter and live from my brush."

The director said, "I think you have the ability to be a painter within you. I hope that you will develop yourself."

Pancho happened to think of Juana. "I," he boasted, "have a model now and am sketching her in the nude!"

Old Aguirre said thoughtfully, "It is a good idea to have a model. With practice in class and out of class, you will grow more sure of yourself. . . ."

Pancho was full of hope when he climbed up to the roof

that night. A tablet of drawing paper and several pencils were tucked under his coat.

Juana whispered, "I was in the kitchen and heard what your mother said about drawing women in their bare flesh." She pointed to a new candle which she had lit before her picture of the Virgin of Guadalupe. "I am praying that the Virgin will not let your mother find out you drew me."

Pancho said, "I want to draw you again."

Juana shuddered. "If your mother found out, she would send me back to my village. My godmother would call me a shameful creature and refuse to allow me in her hut. I would have nowhere in the world to go because the chief of my village took away our hut when my father died."

Pancho tossed his head and cried, "We do nothing wrong! Twice a week I draw a woman's body at art school."

Juana gazed unbelievingly at him.

"If you do not believe me, look. . . ." He drew a picture of the Mexican woman who modeled for Old Aguirre's class.

Juana stared at the picture a long time before she nodded and mumbled, "Well, it must be all right."

She undressed and he began to sketch her slowly. As the evening wore on, he drew her three times but did not like any of the sketches. He felt vexed when he glanced from her body to the bodies on his paper. Juana had firm breasts, curved hips, and slim legs the color of bronze. Pancho saw that he had drawn one hip larger than the other and made her breasts sag. He became so angry with the sketches that he broke his pencil in half.

Juana was looking at the ceiling and thought he broke his pencil by chance. She dropped her eyes and exclaimed, "What a pity!"

Pancho paid no heed to Juana and strode furiously up and

down the room. He pushed out his bottom lip and pouted because he had drawn such hideous sketches of her beautiful body.

Juana wrapped her black shawl around her body and watched Pancho walk the floor. When his footsteps sounded very heavy, she whispered "Don Pancho, you are making too much noise. Someone might hear and tell your mother that a man is walking in my room."

"Nonsense!" he said to take away her fear. But his stomach felt empty when he looked at her and thought: How horrible it would be if my mother sent Juana back to her village and I could never draw her again. . . .

He asked nervously, "Juana, do you have a newspaper?"

She fetched an old paper that she hoarded underneath her straw mat.

Pancho unfolded the newspaper and carefully laid his sketches between the pages. He reflected grimly: My sketches are bad, but I must hide them from my mother . . . if she saw them, she might suspect that I draw Juana. . . .

As he climbed down from the roof, he hugged the paper to his chest and said to himself: These sketches are mine and Juana is mine to draw . . . I must be careful and keep this secret from my mother as if it were my life. . . .

For many nights he was cautious so that his mother would not find out the secret. He waited until she retired for the evening. Then he hid behind her bedroom and listened while she unhooked her corset. When her mattress creaked, he climbed up the stairway and slipped into Juana's room.

He forgot his mother the minute he began to draw Juana. All of his energy went into his pencil, but he drew as slowly as if he had his whole life to do one sketch. He took great pains and labored for hours to make Juana's body as beautiful as it was. Every time he finished a sketch, he felt discontented. Her body always seemed crude and ugly on his paper.

Summer flew by while he drew Juana over and over. The days grew colder and the wind blew dry leaves off the trees. One night in November, he went to Juana's room earlier than usual to put the last touches on a sketch. When he finished it, his eyes darted uneasily from her body to the body he had drawn. Suddenly he sighed so loud that the fat on his chest heaved.

A warm glow spread through his body and rose to his head. Sweat broke out on his forehead and wet the hair that had fallen over it. Pancho laughed and cried, "I did it! I caught the beauty of her body on paper!" He pored over the sketch and rubbed his hands together from satisfaction.

Pancho felt as though he had made a great discovery because Juana was the first woman he had ever drawn with beauty. He was so happy that he strutted around the room and shouted to Juana, "Now that I have drawn you, I will paint you in beautiful colors! Bronze for your body! Ebony black for your hair and crimson for your lips. . . ."

Someone rapped on the door and called, "Juana! Juana!"

She grabbed her black shawl as an old woman with a shriveled brown face came into the room. It was her godmother. The old woman looked at her godchild's bare body and shrieked, *"Dios!"* Her long black dress swished as she ran to the stairway and howled, *"Señora Pacheco! Señor Pacheco!"*

Pancho's mother and father rushed into the room.

His mother flung her hands to her face when she saw Juana clad only in her black shawl and screamed, "Evil! Sinful children!"

Tears flowed from Juana's eyes while Pancho shouted with

fury, "What did she do wrong? I begged her to let me draw her naked and she let me!"

"You are a wicked boy!" his mother cried at him.

His father stared down at Juana's straw mat. It was strewn with her clothes, pencils, and paper. He pleaded to his wife, "They are innocent children. Pancho is drawing Juana's body. . . ."

Pancho's mother said, "I will not have that girl in my house any longer! She must go back to her village!"

The godmother shook her finger at Juana and spat out, "She is a shameless creature! I will not let her in the door of my hut!"

Juana pulled on a skirt and blouse and covered her head with her black shawl. Tears rolled down her brown face while she wrapped her old clothes and the picture of the Virgin in her faded blue and red blanket. As she went out of the room with the bundle under her arm, she hung her head and wailed, "They have cast me out of their homes . . . and I have nowhere to go. . . ."

Pancho knew that he would never draw Juana again. He yelled at his mother, "I hate you! I wish you were dead!"

REVOLT

REVOLT

HE WAS WALKING across the main plaza in Mexico City
when he saw a barefoot woman, with a dark red shawl
wrapped around her head and shoulders, roasting a few ears
of corn on a charcoal brazier. She looked timidly at him out
of the corners of her black eyes and hoped that he would buy
some of her corn. He sniffed at it and thought: The corn does
not smell very good . . . but how could it . . . after being in
bed so many days with a cold. . . . I always liked to eat hot
corn on the plaza . . . but it does not tempt me now.

The woman stooped over her brazier and fanned her charcoal into flames with a piece of straw when he walked away.
His nose began to drip while he stood on the edge of the plaza
and waited for a carriage to pass before he crossed the street.
He felt peevish as he turned down a narrow street that led to
the school of art and he grumbled: I, Pancho Pacheco, am
sixteen years old . . . for almost four years I have studied art
. . . now I am tired of being an art student . . . my classes in
the school are stupid and bore me.

A lean yellow dog ran by him with its tail between its legs
while he thought: Life is beautiful but short . . . I only want
to do things that give me pleasure . . . it must be pretty in the
country now . . . I would like to go to some village and paint
hills and trees from morning until night . . . I wish that I had

111

my freedom and did not have to study in the school another night.

He glanced at an old clock in a little shop that sold bibles, crosses, and pictures of the saints. It was six o'clock in the evening. For a few minutes he looked absent-mindedly into the shop and saw nothing while he meditated: I do not know why I am going to art school . . . except that I am sick and tired of staying in bed . . . I could go to a cheap cafe and drink a cup of tea . . . but since I am so close to the school and have my drawing paper and books with me, I might as well go. . . .

A crippled old man who begged for money on the streets watched Pancho walk into the school of art. He was shocked when he saw hundreds of art students congregated in the patio of the school. They were talking in small groups and had crowded around two huge paintings with gold frames that hung on the wall. The sound of the boys' voices filled his ears like the waves of a rough sea. He heard several boys say, "Those paintings are no good! Bah! There is nothing modern in his paintings!" He pushed his way toward some boys whom he knew.

A boy named Carlos slapped him on the back and cried, "Where have you been, Pancho?"

"In bed with a bad cold," he said.

Another boy called Pepe asked, "Did you read about him in the newspapers?"

"I had too much fever to read," said Pancho impatiently. "What," he waved at the crowds, "is going on here? Whom are you talking about?"

"About the new director!" Pepe said.

"New director?" Pancho blurted out. "What happened to Old Aguirre?"

"He was retired," said Carlos angrily, "because he is supposed to be too old-fashioned! A few days ago a painter from Europe, whom none of us knows, was made our director for the purpose of modernizing the school."

"But it was unjust to retire Old Aguirre," Pancho protested. "The old man has been the director of our school for as long as I can remember."

"Surely it was unjust to retire him," said a boy named Jesús. "I have no desire to hear the speech that our new director will make to us tonight. In honor of the occasion, two of his paintings were hung up this morning."

Pancho stared at the pictures and jeered, "Those paintings of Moors and of knights are not modern! Our new director paints about the dark ages like any old European hack." Pancho held his nose. "Fuf, the paintings stink! The only thing good about them are the gold frames."

All the boys except Pepe laughed and cried, "You are right!"

Pepe said, "You talk like a madman, Pancho! The painter from Europe is more modern than Old Aguirre. It was time for him to be retired. He is an old fool of seventy-seven years. . . ."

Pancho shouted at Pepe, "Shut up! Old Aguirre was the best director that our school ever had."

The other boys cried out, "Yes sir, Old Aguirre was a great director!"

Carlos said tartly, "Pepe is happy because Old Aguirre is leaving us."

Pepe's face turned red as someone yelled, "Quiet!"

The noise in the patio subsided gradually. When all the boys raised their heads, Pancho looked up and saw Old Aguirre walking down the stairway that led into the patio.

He was resting one hand on the banister and holding a black hat in his other hand. His white head was high in the air and he carried himself very erectly. He wore a black cape over a black suit that made his corpulent body look stately.

A crowd of boys flocked after Pancho when he rushed upstairs to shake hands with the old man. All the other students in the patio followed the crowd and mobbed up the stairway to tell their old director goodbye. They poked and punched one another in the back and tried to get close to Old Aguirre. His spectacles grew misty as he shook hands with boy after boy.

Carlos said, "It is a shame you are going away, Master!"

Another boy cried, "We will miss you terribly, Master!"

Pancho squeezed the old man's hand and said, "I will never forget that you were the first teacher who encouraged me to be a painter."

Old Aguirre patted Pancho's shoulder. "Keep on painting, Pacheco, and let nothing stop you! I feel that you might be a good painter someday."

Pancho was so happy that he spluttered his thanks to the Master.

Pepe looked enviously at Pancho and thought: I am glad that Old Aguirre will soon be gone . . . he is always telling Pancho how good his work is . . . but that boy cannot paint any better than the rest of us. . . .

Jesús stepped on Pancho's feet while he shook the old director's hand and cried huskily, "We do not want you to go, Master!"

Old Aguirre said, "It is too bad that I must leave you boys. I love the school and I love every one of you. But I, as an individual, do not count. It is the school which counts now. If I have been deemed too old in years and too old-fashioned in my art for the school, then I think that a younger and a more modern man should succeed me."

Pancho stared at the sad faces of the boys around him and thought: They feel the same way that I feel . . . Old Aguirre has been our director for so many years that we always believed he would be with us until the day of his death . . . now Old Aguirre has been retired and he is not protesting nor fussing because a painter from Europe was put in our school to take his place.

Old Aguirre tried to joke. "My boys, I am not a mosquito who can fly through this mob. . . ." He ran his eyes over the stairway. It was packed with boys and he could not take a step. "The hour has come for me to go. . . ."

The boys pushed one another down the steps to make room for Old Aguirre. Within a few minutes they cleared the whole stairway for him. As he walked slowly down the steps, the boys turned their heads away or looked down at the floor to hide their feelings of sympathy for him. When he came to the bottom of the stairway, they crowded against the sides of the door to say goodbye to him for the last time. The old director smiled and nodded at the boys while he walked out of the patio to the sidewalk.

Just as he was about to step into his carriage, a little fellow ran out on the street and cried at him, "I do not want a foreign director!"

Old Aguirre stepped back from the carriage when he saw all of the students in the patio crowd out on the sidewalk. They mobbed around the carriage and even held the door so that the old man could not drive away.

Pancho howled, "Nobody wants a new director!"

Carlos yelled, "We want Aguirre!"

Many boys shouted, "We do not want a foreigner for our

Pancho stood beside the old director while he laid his hand over his heart and said goodbye to the boys

director!" The shouts were so loud that they could be heard
the length of the street. Jesús cried in a shrill voice, "We
want justice!" The cry was taken up by other boys and rent
the air until Old Aguirre waved his hand for silence.

"My boys," the old director said firmly, "it has been decided that I should retire in favor of the painter from Europe.
I think that the decision is entirely just."

Pancho thought suspiciously: Old Aguirre was not retired
because he is old-fashioned. . . .

Old Aguirre said, "The new director has taught for years
in an old academy in Spain, and his paintings are well known
in Europe. I believe that he will be a fine director and do his
best to modernize the school. I hope that you remember to
treat him with the same consideration which you gave me and
that you will always keep the welfare of the school in your
minds."

He put on his hat and took a step toward the carriage.
Pancho walked up to Old Aguirre and stood beside him, wish-
ing that he were not going away. The old director was so
corpulent that Pancho looked small beside him.

Old Aguirre said kindly, "Good evening, my boys," and
laid his hand over his heart, "may God bless all of you." He
stepped into the carriage and it rolled down the street.

The boys pushed and shoved one another as they crowded
back into the patio from the sidewalk. They said in loud
voices, "Poor Old Aguirre. . . . It is a pity. . . . He was a
better director than the foreign painter will ever be. . . ."

Pancho raged to Carlos, "It is a dirty lie that the foreigner
was brought to modernize our school! Anybody can see from
his old paintings of Moors and knights that he will never
modernize us!"

Many boys heard Pancho and became excited. They

crowded around him, waving their hands and talking at the same time. Carlos shouted, "I agree with you, Pancho! It is a filthy lie that he came to modernize the school!" Another boy cried, "His paintings smell like old cheese!"

Pancho exploded, "I believe that Old Aguirre was retired because he is a Mexican! You know that foreign artists are liked better than Mexican artists in these times. I think that the foreigner was made our director simply because he comes from an academy in Spain and is known in Europe. . . ."

Jesús interrupted, "You are right! In these times foreigners are liked better than our own people! Everybody knows that our President Don Porfirio Diaz lets rich Spanish and English companies exploit our people and our best silver mines and oil wells!"

Pancho raved, "This is not the first time that a foreign artist was invited to Mexico! Two years ago a bad artist was brought from Italy to design our opera house. When it is finished it will look like a white elephant with a round brass hat on its head! Now this old-fashioned painter has been imported from Spain to be our director!"

The boys listened, nodded their heads and said to one another, "Pancho Pacheco speaks the truth. . . . Foreign artists have all the privileges now. . . ."

Pepe looked at Pancho and thought: That boy is crazy and I hate him . . . I wish that the new director could hear what he is saying . . . he would get angry and might kick Pancho out of the school. . . .

Pancho said, "Maybe we will never have any more liberty because the new director might try to make our school into a Spanish academy and treat our old teachers as badly as Old Aguirre has been treated!"

The bell rang.

Somebody cried, "It is time for him to make his speech!"

Pancho shouted, "Let us go hear what that man has to say!"

All the boys crowded out of the patio and moved toward the lecture hall. As they tramped down the corridor, many students talked angrily against the new director. One fellow said, "Who knows why Old Aguirre was retired, but it is not right!" Another boy cried, "Right is might! The board makes a foreigner our director, and what can we do about it?"

The boys poured into the lecture hall and grabbed for chairs. Most of them stopped talking when they were seated. A taut silence, like the quiet before a storm, spread through the hall for several minutes. Some fellow, sitting in a back seat, broke the silence by whispering loud, "Here he is!"

Everybody turned around to see the new director. He wore a black suit that made him look tall and pompous. The light shone on his ruddy hatchet-face and pointed blond beard as he walked up the aisle with his aquiline nose in the air. He stepped on the dais, bowed politely to the students, and said, "Good evening, gentlemen. I am happy to be with you tonight and consider it a privilege because I, a Spaniard," he opened his gray eyes wider and raised his voice, "was appointed the director of the school."

A group of boys sat on the edge of their chairs and mumbled to one another, "He thinks that he is better than us because he is a Spaniard. . . . Listen to him show off his Castilian Spanish. . . . He thinks he talks purer Spanish than we talk in Mexico. . . . Look at him walk like a rooster. . . ."

The Master strutted up and down the dais and said, "To my mind this school is not only a center of art but is a reflection of the great progress and foreign culture which President Porfirio Diaz has brought to Mexico."

Pancho said to himself: I would like to do something to that idiot and get Old Aguirre back in the school. . . .

The painter from Spain said, "I hope, while I am director of your school, that you boys will drink as deeply of Spanish art as your great grandfathers did when Mexico was a colony of Spain. Although Mexico is now a republic, I am sure you realize that you must continue to seek most of your inspiration from Spanish art because art has flourished for many centuries in Spain whereas Mexico is in the New World and has no art of her own except the primitive art of Indians which can hardly be called art."

Angry whispers, mutters, and exclamations came from the boys. Carlos said half aloud, "The art of our Indians is primitive but more beautiful than the art of Spanish painters like him. . . ." A boy growled, "I would like to murder the Spaniards who conquered our Indians and made our country a colony of Spain!" Somebody mumbled, "The Spaniards killed and robbed our Indians!" A fellow whined, "Now a Spaniard is robbing us of our director. . . ." Jesús muttered, "We ought to ship that fool back to Spain where he belongs!"

Pancho thought: All the boys hate the Spaniard . . . it would be easy to get them to strike. . . .

"I am very glad," said the Master, "that I was appointed director of your school for the purpose of modernizing it. I intend to bring the techniques which are being taught, in these first years of the twentieth century, in Spanish academies to your school. I believe that you should also become acquainted with the modern art of Spain. Two paintings by me are now hanging on the walls of your patio. The paintings are modern. . . ."

"Modern like the pants of my grandfather!" Carlos shrieked.

Pancho fingered a box of matches in his pocket and said to himself: I will show him what we Mexicans can do to bad paintings. . . .

All the boys started to whistle, hiss, and scrape their feet at the new director. He bowed stiffly to his audience, stepped off the dais, and strode up the aisle to the door. As he disappeared into his office, he blew his nose furiously and thought: These Mexican boys act like savages. . . .

The boys talked against their new director and called him dirty names while they jammed the aisles and crowded toward the door. Pancho shouted, "We must strike against that man!" Everybody turned around and crowded back into the hall. Carlos jumped on a chair and screamed, "I am ready!" Another boy yelled, "Down with the foreigner!" Jesús shook his fists and howled, "Down with the Spaniard!" Many boys waved their right arms, pounded the floor with their feet, and screamed, "We are for the strike!"

Pancho shouted, "You must refuse to come to any class until Old Aguirre is reinstated as our director. . . ." All the boys threw their caps in the air, whistled, and hollered, "Up with Old Aguirre! We are for Aguirre and the strike! We will not go to our classes until Old Aguirre comes back!"

The boys made so much noise that Pancho could not finish what he had to say. He roared, "Shut up a minute, boys, and listen to me!"

Pepe cried out, "What right have you to command us?" Another boy shrieked, "Pancho Pacheco thinks that he is President Porfirio Diaz!" Carlos yelled, "Let Pancho talk! He thought up the strike!"

Pancho said at the top of his voice, "We must begin the strike with a big fire and burn up those paintings by him!"

Many boys hollered, "That is a good idea! We want to do

it! We will do it tonight!" Jesús cried, "We should burn up those paintings and throw that Spaniard into the fire!" A tall fellow stood on the dais and shouted, "Why can't we make the fire in the patio?" "Let's go to the patio! What are we waiting for? Let's make the fire now!" came from the rest.

One little fellow bawled, "Where can we get wood for the fire?"

Carlos picked up his chair and screamed, "We can use the chairs!"

All the boys except Pepe grabbed a chair or two from the lecture hall. Holding the chairs above their heads, they crowded together and pushed out of the door. The legs of the chairs rocked in the air and caught together as the mob of students tramped down the corridor to the patio. Jesús ran into some classrooms, on the way to the patio, and stole the waste paper baskets. In the excitement no one noticed that Pepe's hands were empty.

The boys were mobbing the patio with their chairs and railing against the new director when two old teachers walked in the door of the school. They took a look at the riot, stepped out on the sidewalk, and whispered to each other, "The students are rebelling against *him*. . . . Maybe they can get Old Aguirre reinstated. . . . That would be a miracle. . . . None of the teachers want *him* to be our director. . . . But you know that we can do nothing. . . ."

The teachers smiled while the boys piled up the chairs in the middle of the patio. Jesús scattered his waste paper under the rungs and lit the fire. Many fellows crowded around Pancho when he climbed on a chair to pull down the gold-framed paintings. As he tore the knights off the wall, he swore, "To hell with this old garbage!" Carlos jerked both of his thumbs at the knights and grabbed the picture out of Pancho's hands.

He made a queer noise as he pulled down the other painting of the Moors.

Flames were curling around the chairs and leaping toward the ceiling of the patio. Somebody yelled, "Burn up the Moors! Burn up the knights!" when Pancho and Carlos shoved the paintings into the fire. The flames lashed at the gold frames while the Moors' turbans and the knights' red-hilted swords glared in the bright light. The boys whistled and jeered at the old paintings and crowded around the fire to watch them burn.

Pepe sneaked out of the patio and ran to the office of the new director as a boy shrieked, "The behinds of the Moors have caught on fire!" Another boy cried, "The guts of the knights are burning up!" Within a few minutes the gold frames darkened and cracked and the colors in the paintings turned coal black. One picture fell apart from its frame and was crumbling to ashes when a firewagon drawn by horses stopped in front of the school.

The teachers walked across the street when the firemen dragged a hose into the patio. Some boy saw the firemen first and howled, "Take the hose away from them!" A gang of boys tried to grab the hose while others watched the fight and yelled, "Pull it harder! Hold on to it!" The firemen wrenched the hose away from the boys and turned the water on all of them.

As the men killed the fire, they cursed at the students, "You are bums! We should take you to jail for trying to burn up the school!"

The fire was dead when the new director walked into the patio. His face became the color of a ripe tomato while he stared at the ashes and scorched remains of his art. He shouted at the students, "You have destroyed two of my best paintings! What barbarians you Mexicans are!"

Jesús took a step toward him and yelled, "We are not barbarians! We are good Mexicans!" A great number of boys frowned and clenched their fists.

"I know," the Master cried, "the name of the person who started this riot and I am going to expel him!"

Pancho sneezed because he was standing in a pool of water.

"This school of art," said the painter from Spain in a harsh voice, "has no space for a boy known as Pancho Pacheco!"

Carlos muttered, "What a bastard he is. . . ." The rest of the boys looked from the new director to Pancho and dropped their eyes guiltily.

"Neither," said the Master, "has the school any space for the other boys who helped Pacheco to start the fire: Carlos Zeta, Jesús de la . . ."

Pancho walked out of the school. His nose was dripping and his nostrils quivered while he thought: Some boy went to that man and told him who led the strike . . . who could it have been . . . everybody was for Old Aguirre except Pepe . . . that boy has always been jealous of me . . . I think he did it.

The cathedral bells were pealing nine o'clock. He listened to the time and said to himself: Three hours ago I wished that I did not have to study in the art school anymore . . . the son of a dog gave me freedom when he expelled me . . . now I can go to the country and paint hills and trees all day long.

Pancho laughed and strode down the street. He was a free man.

THE LITTLE GENERAL

THE LITTLE GENERAL

ONE NIGHT a band of young men were playing music on the sidewalk of a restaurant in Mexico City. The restaurant was in a tall old stone edifice with balconies, and its name was printed boldly above the door in black letters: LE MONTPARNASSE. All the musicians wore derbies, high white collars, and dark suits with short coats and tight pants. They stood up very stiffly while they sang and played love songs which were popular in Paris and dreamy waltzes by Mexican composers on guitars, violins, and a cello.

When the musicians finished playing a waltz, one of them took off his derby and walked into the Montparnasse. That night it was crowded with Mexican bohemians and singers and dancers who had come to town with an Italian opera company. Small tin lamps hung beside the tables and cast a dim light on the faces of people who were eating. Waiters carrying trays of food in their hands brushed past the old tapestries from France, which decorated the walls, as they rushed hither and thither to serve the guests.

The musician went from table to table and passed around his derby until he came to a crowd of Mexican painters who were drinking wine. One of them had a beard which grew around his cheeks and a goatee. He was a painter, called Don Agustín, who owned a small art gallery. When he saw the musician, he tossed a coin into his derby. The musician said,

"Gracias, señor!" and went up to some Italian singers who were talking in loud voices.

Don Agustín stroked his goatee while he listened to a tale which a big-bellied painter, who sat opposite him, was telling the other painters. As he talked, he pushed his chair away from the table to make room for his belly. He wore a navy blue suit that was stained with paint, wrinkled, and fit him so badly his fat seemed to burst out of it. "Last night," he said in a boastful voice, "I went to a cabaret that was full of old women and girls. When the girls saw me come in the door, they crowded around me. . . ."

The other painters looked at his ugly but attractive face. His long dark hair was tangled over his ears and hung over his forehead. He had black eyes, which bulged like those of a frog, and a wide pug nose. His fleshy, sensuous mouth was framed by a beard that curled around his jowls. "One girl," he laughed, "fell in love with me and began to fight with the rest of the girls. She pulled their hair and scratched their arms and faces until they let her take me to a table in a corner. . . ."

He paused for a minute and licked his lips. "I sat there all night, drinking beer and making love to her, and did not leave until dawn. Maybe I will make love to her another night because she was very beautiful. She had on a rose colored dress and her figure was like this. . . ." He sketched her figure on a napkin and showed it to the painters. They looked at the sketch and believed the story because the girl sounded real enough. The only man who smiled, as though he doubted the tale, was Don Agustín.

The big-bellied painter reached across the table for the bottle of wine, put it up to his mouth, and threw back his head. As he drained the bottle, wine trickled down his chin and wet the hair around his jowls. The other men laughed and clapped their hands for a waiter to bring another bottle.

Wine and food were brought to the table while a painter said, "Last night I went to see La Marie dance at the theater. She is wonderful!"

"Without doubt," some painter said, "La Marie is the most beautiful dancer who ever came here on a tour. Her face is as marvelous as her body."

The painter who had told the cabaret story listened avidly to the talk about La Marie for a few seconds. Then his black pop eyes darted around the table and rested on the food that was getting cold. He bent his head over his plate and swallowed down his dinner greedily. When he finished it, he was still hungry. He emptied a bowl of rice, which belonged to a painter next to him, into his plate. The painters went on talking about La Marie while he ate up all the bread on the table and even the chiles in vinegar.

As he loosened his belt and leaned back, a leg of his chair broke. He rose clumsily to his feet and the chair fell on the floor. All the painters laughed, and people turned around to look. An Italian soprano, wearing a long gray dress and a big hat trimmed with white aigrettes, giggled very loudly.

A painter cried, "When Pancho sells another painting, he will have to buy a chair for the Montparnasse!"

A little painter said, "Maybe some people say that Pancho Pacheco is a great artist because he weighs hundreds of pounds!"

Shame filled Pancho because he was fat, but he threw out his chest and laughed. He even joked so that his friends would not guess how inferior his size made him feel. "My mother used to call me Pancho . . ." he said drolly. "Now I use the great name, which my mother gave me when I was born, to fit my height. . . ." He rolled off a long name, "Francisco María de la Concepción de Pacheco y Rodriguez!"

Don Agustín and the rest of the painters laughed.

"For short," he cried arrogantly, "I am Don Pancho Pacheco!" He picked up his wide-brimmed hat and bowed slightly. "Good evening, gentlemen!"

He swaggered out of the Montparnasse with his head in the air. When he passed the musicians, he pulled his hat over his eyes and walked slowly down the street. He seemed to hear the giggle of the Italian soprano in his ears, and he flung out his hands as though he wished to push her out of his mind. A strong hatred of his flesh spread through him while he thought: I am a man now . . . twenty years old . . . my face is ugly and I am as fat as a pig.

His chest felt heavy and he sighed as if he were overcome by sorrow. He brooded: No woman has ever fallen in love with me . . . all the women I know stay away from me or laugh at me . . . some of them even look at me with an expression in their eyes that says, "Who is that ugly giant?" . . . but at least no one knows that I do not have a sweetheart . . . because I make up stories about what a great lover I am . . . and all the world believes my stories.

He put his hand in his coat pocket and pulled out a torn old handkerchief. As he blew his nose, he mused: I might be fat and ugly . . . but someday I will be a great painter . . . maybe the greatest one in Mexico . . . even now the old painters say I have much talent . . . and all the young painters are jealous because I sell the most paintings.

Don Pancho tossed his head and whistled as a night watchman, carrying a lantern in his hand, hurried past him. He thought: I am too tired to take a walk . . . and I do not feel like going to my studio and painting . . . tonight my friends talked so much about La Marie that I am curious . . . she must be a beautiful woman . . . I will go to the theater now and see her dance.

He strolled up the street until the lights of the theater glimmered before him. When he saw the price of the tickets, he mumbled, "Barbarous!" His dome-shaped forehead wrinkled up while he thought of the long hours he worked on his paintings so that they would sell. A picture of La Marie, as he imagined her, loomed up in his mind. He smiled from anticipation, dug into his pocket for some money, and bought a ticket to the top gallery.

Breathing heavily, he climbed up a narrow stairway that led to the gallery. He stumbled on the last step, reeled, and caught his balance. A vile oath left his mouth while he groped for a seat. He finally sat down in front of a crowd of school girls who began to scream, "*Su sombrero! No podemos ver nada por su sombrero grandote!* His hat's so big we can't see!"

He winced and took off his hat. As the curtain went up, he folded his hands on his belly. He forgot the girls when the show began. . . .

The pudgy conductor of the orchestra bowed his head and waved his baton. Sublime music of flutes and violins floated through the theater and soared as La Marie danced across the stage on her toes. Golden hair streamed down her back, and her skin was snow-white. The silver spangles on her pink ballet skirt twinkled in the bright stage-lights. Her white silk stockings gleamed when she whirled around with her arms gracefully arched in the air.

Don Pancho whispered, "Marvelous . . . her legs are marvelous. . . ."

She wove a spell around him while she danced. The colors

131

of her costumes quickly changed from pink to rose to purple to crimson and dazzled him. Waves of heat rose from his belly and cold perspiration broke out on his forehead when she pirouetted. Her body pulsated with the rapid music and made his head spin as though he were very drunk. She intoxicated him more than the whole bottle of wine he had drunk in the Montparnasse.

The magic spell lasted until midnight. When the curtain fell, loud applause came from the audience. Don Pancho looked down at the audience while he clapped as hard as he could. A row of young *catrines* or dandies, who loafed on their father's money, were sitting in front of the stage. They had been staring at La Marie's legs through gold and silver opera glasses which they held in their hands. Their high white collars shone as they turned their heads and gossiped to one another about her performance.

When the curtain rose again, La Marie had a large bouquet of pink roses in her arms. She curtsied and smiled and curtsied at the audience.

Don Pancho saw a general, in a box near the stage, clapping very loudly, bowing from the waist, and smiling broadly at La Marie. He thought: Maybe the General gave La Marie the roses because he is in love with her. . . .

The General had a white mustache which curled halfway across his cheeks, a hooked nose, and small black eyes that were as sharp as an eagle's. He looked very short in his blue coat, with gold epaulets on his shoulders, and white trousers. His broad chest was decorated with so many gold and silver medals and bright ribbons that it glittered like a Christmas tree. He carried a pistol on his hip and a sword hung down his left side.

All of a sudden Don Pancho recognized the General from

pictures he had seen in the newspapers. He was General Fulano de Tal, the shortest general in the Mexican Army but the most clever politician in Mexico. The little General was so clever that the Dictator of Mexico, Don Porfirio Diaz, made him a diplomat and sent him on special missions to Washington for the purpose of arranging a friendly policy between Mexico and the United States.

The applause faded as the curtain was lowered on La Marie. People crowded out of the gallery and Don Pancho lumbered down the stairway behind them. His lips were pouted and he thought crossly: My seat was so high up that I could not see her face. . . . As he went out of the theater, he saw many dandies, carrying top hats, flowers, and candy, pouring into a corridor that led backstage. He followed them with the hope that he might see La Marie.

The dandies' frock coats swished while they pushed one another down the corridor. When they reached La Marie's dressing-room, they craned their necks and peered into it. Within a few minutes she came to the door and smiled at her admirers. Her teeth were like pearls and her eyes blue as the sea. She wore a purple velvet dress, which swept the floor, and a large hat trimmed with ostrich plumes. A white ermine scarf was around her shoulders.

All the dandies started to rave to La Marie about her performance. Don Pancho longed to tell her that she was beautiful, but he was afraid that she might give him a look which said, "Who is this fat, ugly man?" Something within him shrank when he noticed how slim and handsome the dandies were. They made him feel inferior, and he moved back against the wall while they gave her candy and flowers and cried, "You danced superbly . . . divinely. . . ."

Suddenly the little General strutted past Don Pancho with

133

his broad chest high in the air. He stepped up to La Marie and bowed graciously from his head to his stomach while he kissed her small white hand. She smiled fondly at the General and cried in a lilting voice, *"Bonsoir, mon ami!"* He looked up at her as though he adored her and murmured, *"Buenas noches, linda. . . ."*

Don Pancho stared at the little General and began to feel superior to him. He thought: The General is half as tall as I . . . he looks like a dwarf in comparison to me . . . and his face is uglier than mine . . . I might have eyes like a frog . . . but the General has eyes like a pig . . . and my hair is not white. . . .

All the dandies stepped to one side when General Fulano de Tal took La Marie's arm and led her down the corridor. She was two heads taller than the General and his legs were so short that he had to walk very briskly to keep up with her. Don Pancho grinned and said to himself with a toss of his head: I could easily take La Marie away from that little General. . . .

The dandies talked under their breaths about the General as they crowded out of the corridor to the backstage entrance. For a minute or two Don Pancho stood on the sidewalk with them and watched La Marie and the General drive away from the theater in a carriage. Some of the dandies glanced disdainfully at his paint-smeared clothes, sniffed, and turned up their noses.

When the carriage disappeared, Don Pancho walked slowly to his studio thinking: The General is an old man and probably a coward . . . he would be so afraid of me if he saw me making love to La Marie that he would run like a hare . . . and La Marie and I could go on making love like Romeo and Juliet. . . .

It was nearly two o'clock in the morning when Don Pancho let himself in the door of a gray stone tenement house. He climbed up three flights of stairs until he came to a small room which he used as a studio. The only furniture in the room were a cot, one chair, a table, and an easel. He sank down on the cot and groaned as he took off his black high-topped shoes. . . .

Visions of La Marie floated before his eyes when he sat down to paint in the morning. He forgot about her while he put the last touches on a painting of hills and trees. As he painted, he pushed out his bottom lip and fretted: There is something wrong with this landscape . . . I do not like the form . . . and the colors seem dirty to me . . . the old painters say I am a good painter . . . but I am not satisfied with any of my paintings. . . . He made a face while he signed his name and the year 1906 on a corner of the picture.

Toward noon Don Agustin came to see him. He looked at the painting and said, "I like that. It is nice."

Don Pancho grumbled, "The more I paint the more dissatisfied I become. For four years I have wandered around Mexico painting landscapes, houses, churches, and Indians. Maybe I have learned all I can here in Mexico."

Don Agustín said, "You ought to go to Paris and study there."

"Fuf!" Don Pancho cried. "Where would I get the money to go to Paris?"

Don Agustín said, "I will help you to have a show in my art gallery if you get enough paintings together. People will buy the paintings and, with the money from them, you can pay for the voyage to France."

"It will be a struggle," said Don Pancho slowly, "to earn

135

a living from my painting, while I am studying in Paris, but I want to go. . . ."

All that November and December he painted day and night to get enough paintings together for a show. He wanted to study in Paris so much that La Marie faded out of his mind while he painted. One day at dusk, near the end of the year, he rubbed his eyes and put his palette down. He was tired of painting and wished that he had a sweetheart and could see her now. As he lumbered restlessly up and down his studio, he remembered La Marie and wondered if she were still dancing at the theater.

A newspaper was on his cot, and he turned to the theater page and read, "Gala performance of La Marie tonight. . . ." He smiled and thought: I am going to take La Marie away from that little General . . . I will ask her to let me paint her portrait and make her fall in love with me. . . . He washed the paint off his hands, changed his shirt, and wiped his shoes with a blanket on his cot. Then he put on his old blue coat and picked up his wide-brimmed hat.

It was almost time for La Marie's performance when Don Pancho knocked on the door of her dressing-room. A Frenchman, wearing a diamond stickpin in his cravat and a long black coat, opened the door. He looked at the spots of paint on Don Pancho's pants and said in a snooty voice, "I am Monsieur Philippe Durand, the manager of Mademoiselle Marie. What do you wish?"

Don Pancho took off his hat and said arrogantly, "I am Señor Pacheco, the painter. In a few words, I would like to paint a portrait of La Marie."

Monsieur Durand smiled at him and said, "Please come with me. . . ." He led Don Pancho into La Marie's dressing-room. She was sitting at her vanity table, in a white ballet dress, powdering her tiny nose. When she saw a big fat man in her mirror, she opened her eyes very wide and whirled around.

As Don Pancho bowed graciously to kiss her hand, his torn old handkerchief slipped out of his coatpocket and fell on the floor. La Marie turned up her nose and Monsieur Durand laughed under his breath. Don Pancho swore at himself because he made La Marie think that he was a lout instead of a gentleman.

"Please," she said coldly, "sit down."

He leaned back in a pink satin chair, folded his hands on his belly, and said, "You are so beautiful that I want to paint your portrait."

She was very flattered and cried out excitedly, *"Quelle bonne idée!"*

Monsieur Durand nodded and said to her in French, "I think that the portrait would be fine publicity. We have not had a full house since the Italian company began to put on operas. Maybe," he reflected, "all the people in Mexico would come to see you dance, instead of going to hear the operas, if they saw a picture of the portrait in the newspaper." He turned to Don Pancho and said in Spanish, "I want you to paint her in an unconventional costume that will attract the public."

"Of course," he said, "a costume that will show her beautiful legs!"

La Marie smiled at him and thought: He is fat and ugly but young . . . the old General would be jealous of him . . . but the General will be gone while he paints me . . . he is leaving for Washington tonight on a diplomatic mission. . . .

"You may," she said to Don Pancho, "begin the portrait tomorrow. . . ."

137

When Don Pancho came to paint La Marie, he found her in a pale blue costume that floated around her knees and was as thin as gossamer. He looked at her and wondered how she should pose for him. She tilted her head, stood on her toes, and curved her arms gracefully in the air.

"Your leg," he pointed to her right leg, "hold it up as if you were dancing."

She raised her leg and her skirt whirled above her knees. For a minute or two he stared at her legs and thought they were the most beautiful legs he had ever seen. He felt a great urge to make her legs seem as beautiful in a portrait as they were. As he sat down in a big chair and sketched her face and body roughly, he forgot all about his desire to make her fall in love with him. She did not talk nor move a muscle while she posed for him.

When he was almost finished painting her, he remembered that he wanted to make her fall in love with him. He tried to woo her by telling her long tales about beautiful women who had loved him. La Marie said, *"Oui . . . oui . . ."* and rolled her eyes as if she doubted whether he was telling her the truth. He described the women so vividly that she began to feel jealous of them. She smiled coyly at him and said, *"Cher* Pancho . . ." in a low sweet voice. He felt happy because he thought that he was winning her away from the General.

La Marie became very excited when the portrait was finished. She cried, "It is grand! It looks so much like me! You are a great painter, Pancho!"

Monsieur Durand nodded his chin and said, "The portrait is excellent! I will call a photographer to take a picture of it for the Sunday newspaper."

Don Pancho smiled fondly at La Marie and Monsieur

Durand and strutted around his portrait. Their words, "grand, excellent, great painter," hummed in his ears and intoxicated him more than if he had drunk a case of wine.

"Before I forget," said Monsieur Durand, "go to the ticket-window tomorrow night and you will find a ticket there in an envelope for a box."

As Don Pancho picked up his hat, La Marie held out her hand for him to kiss. "Please," she said, "come to see me tomorrow night before the performance. . . ."

A picture of the portrait came out in the Sunday newspaper and caused a scandal in Mexico City. The wealthy people talked about the portrait all morning long as they drove up and down the fashionable Paseo de la Reforma.

Old and young Mexican ladies, with black lace shawls around their heads, rode down the Paseo after church in closed carriages, saying: "The portrait is by a young painter called Pacheco . . . and it is scandalous . . . she looks almost naked in the portrait . . . but maybe we should go to see her dance. . . ."

The dandies rode up the Paseo in open carriages, with silk hats and flowers in their buttonholes, talking about La Marie's legs in the portrait and on the stage. They did not stop talking until they reached the theater where they bought front-row tickets for her performance that night.

Aristocratic Mexican horsemen, wearing big felt sombreros, short leather jackets trimmed with silver buttons, and tight pantaloons, cantered down the Paseo, thinking about the portrait of La Marie and wanting to see her dance.

Rich Americans and Europeans drove down the Paseo in coaches, asking one another if they had seen La Marie dance. Many of them said, "No, but we will go to see her dance tonight . . . instead of going to the Italian opera. . . ."

That night all the tickets in the theater were sold for La Marie's performance. A mounted policeman had to ride up and down the street to control the crowds of people who poured toward the theater. In the crowds were all the dandies in Mexico City and hundreds of Europeans, Americans, and Mexicans dressed in evening clothes from Paris. They jostled one another and bumped behinds as they pushed into the theater to see La Marie dance.

La Marie was so happy because Don Pancho had made her a sensation that she threw her arms around him, when he walked into her dressing-room before the performance, and cried out in French, "I adore you!"

As he bent his head and kissed her rouged lips, General Fulano de Tal came to the door. He had returned a few hours ago from his diplomatic mission to Washington. When he arrived in Mexico City, he saw the picture of La Marie in the newspaper but thought it was only publicity for her.

Neither La Marie nor Don Pancho saw the little General standing in the doorway. He drew himself up to his full height and glowered at them. His face turned almost purple as he twirled the end of his long white mustache around and around his left forefinger. For a minute he became so enraged from jealousy that he felt as if a mad dog had bitten him. He put his hand on his sword and wished that he could kill his rival. In his imagination he stabbed his rival to death with such fury that he broke his sword and the blade fell at his feet.

La Marie sighed and murmured, "It feels grand to be loved by Pancho Pacheco . . . the greatest painter in Mexico. . . ."

General Fulano de Tal threw back his shoulders and puffed out his chest. His hand slipped off the sword while his eyes roved slowly down the body of Don Pancho. He thought: Pacheco is too big and too much trouble to kill . . . but what

The little General became so enraged from jealousy that he felt as if a
mad dog had bitten him

can I do to stop him from making love to La Marie? The
light shone on a new gold medal, pinned over his heart, while
he pondered. He had been given the medal by Don Porfirio
Diaz for his diplomacy in Washington. All of a sudden he
smiled, tapped his chest, and marched down the corridor.

La Marie kissed Don Pancho and said blithely, "Now it is
time for me to dance! Don't forget to pick up your ticket for
the box. . . ."

Don Pancho blew her a kiss and walked to the backstage
entrance. He started to go around the theater when he saw
the little General standing beside his carriage. The General
came up to him and bowed very politely.

"Señor Pacheco," he said in a flowery Spanish, "I want to
congratulate you for the great portrait that you painted."

Don Pancho smiled warmly at him and said, *"Muchas
gracias, General!"*

"It is a pity," said the General, "that a great artist like
you is living in a country as poor in art as Mexico instead of
some large city in Europe, such as Paris, Rome, or Madrid
where there is an atmosphere of art."

Don Pancho nodded and said, "I have desired for several
months to go to Paris and study there."

The General smiled and said, "Let us take a drive through
the streets. . . ." He held open the door of his carriage and
Don Pancho stepped into it. As they drove away from the
theater, the General said, "It would give me pleasure if you
would accept a small pension from me to paint in Paris."

Don Pancho thought: I will not have to struggle to earn a
living while I am studying in Paris. . . . He said very excitedly
to the General, "It is extremely kind of you to offer me a
pension!"

The General took out his wallet and gave him a stack of

pesos. "These will be enough for the journey," he said. "I will send you money every month for your living expenses in care of the Mexican Legation in Paris."

Don Pancho shook the little General's hand and said, "I hope to send you paintings from France in appreciation for the help which you are giving me."

The General thanked him and asked, "Where would you care to go now?"

"I should go home," he said, "to make arrangements for my journey."

The little General put his arms around Don Pancho and wished him a happy voyage when he left him at the door of his studio. As Don Pancho watched the carriage roll down the street, he suddenly realized that the General gave him the pension to get him out of the way of La Marie. Something within him shrank when he thought a little General like that had outwitted him. He became more and more peeved while he climbed up the stairs to his studio thinking: The General was so clever that he did not even mention La Marie. . . .

When he walked into his studio, he found Don Agustín waiting for him. He said, "I came over here to talk to you about your portrait of La Marie."

Don Pancho said glibly, "I never knew that a general was in love with La Marie until this morning. When I went downstairs, a general twice as tall and fat as myself kidnapped me in his carriage and took me to a hut in the mountains. He said to me, 'La Marie has fallen in love with you and wants to leave me for you. I want you to get out of here so that she can forget you, and I am going to give you the money to go to Paris . . .' " Don Pancho paused.

Don Agustín stroked his goatee and smiled as if he thought Don Pancho were telling him a story. The smile left his lips,

and his face became very glum when his friend showed him
the money which the General had given him.

"I became frightened," Don Pancho continued, "when the
General threatened me with his pistol and said, 'I will give
you until midnight to take a train for Veracruz where you can
get on a ship. My aides are watching La Marie and if you
make any attempt to see her before you go, they will kill
you!'"

Don Agustín fell on his knees beside Don Pancho's cot and
pulled out an old valise. "Give me your things," he cried,
"and I will help you pack!" He threw his friend's clothes
and paints into the valise and ran down the stairs ahead of
him to hail a carriage.

As they drove up the street to the depot, Don Pancho
leaned back in his seat and relaxed for the first time in many
hours. "I am so happy," he cried, "that I can study in Paris!"

Don Agustín clasped his hand affectionately and said,
"Good luck to you!"

Don Pancho said, "I suppose this is goodbye. . . ." All of a
sudden he yelled at the coachman, "Stop! Stop!"

"Stop? For what?" asked Don Agustín.

"I forgot to tell La Marie goodbye!"

Don Agustín shouted, "Have you gone mad? The General's
aides will kill you if you tell her goodbye!"

Don Pancho was caught in his lie. He pouted and sighed,
"Adios, Marie. . . ."

Date Due

Demco 293-5			